The Throg task force struck the Terran Survey camp a few minutes after dawn, without warning, and with a deadly precision which argued that the aliens had fully reconnoitered and prepared that attack. Eye-searing lances of energy lashed back and forth across the base with methodical accuracy. And a single cowering witness, flattened on a ledge in the heights above, knew that when the last of those yellow-red bolts fell, nothing human would be left alive. . . .

STORM OVER WARLOCK

ANDRE NORTON

SF
ace books
A Division of Charter Communications Inc.
A GROSSET & DUNLAP COMPANY
51 Madison Avenue
New York, New York 10010

This Ace printing: August 1981

4 6 8 0 9 7 5 3
Manufactured in the United States of America

1. DISASTER

THE Throg task force struck the Terran Survey camp a few minutes after dawn, without warning, and with a deadly precision which argued that the aliens had fully reconnoitered and prepared that attack. Eye-searing lances of energy lashed back and forth across the base with methodical accuracy. And a single cowering witness, flattened on a ledge in the heights above, knew that when the last of those yellow-red bolts fell, nothing human would be left alive down there. His teeth closed hard upon the thick stuff of the sleeve covering his thin forearm, and in his throat a scream of terror and rage was stillborn.

More than caution kept him pinned on that narrow shelf of rock. Watching that holocaust below, Shann Lantee could not force himself to move. The sheer ruthlessness of the Throg move-in left him momentarily weak. To listen to a tale of Throgs in action, and to be an eye-witness to such action, were two vastly different things. He shivered in spite of the warmth of the Survey Corps uniform.

As yet he had sighted none of the aliens, only their plateshaped flyers. They would stay aloft until their long-range weapon cleared out all opposition. But how had they been able to make such a complete annihilation of the Terran force? The last report had placed the nearest

1

Throg nest at least two systems away from Warlock. And a patrol lane had been drawn about the Circe system the minute that Survey had marked its second planet ready for colonization. Somehow the beetles had slipped through that supposedly tight cordon and would now consolidate their gains with their usual speed at rooting. First an energy attack to finish the small Terran force; then they would simply take over.

A month later, or maybe two months, and they could not have done it. The grids would have been up, and any Throg ship venturing into Warlock's amber-tinted sky would abruptly cease to be. In the race for survival as a galactic power, Terra had that one small edge over the swarms of the enemy. They need only stake out their new-found world and get the grids assembled on its surface; then that planet would be locked to the beetles. The critical period was between the first discovery of a suitable colony world and the erection of grid control. Planets in the past had been lost during that time lag, just as Warlock was lost now.

Throgs and Terrans . . . For more than a century now, planet time, they had been fighting their queer, twisted war among the stars. Terrans hunted worlds for colonization, the old hunger for land of their own driving men from the overpopulated worlds, out of Sol's system to the far stars. And those worlds barren of intelligent native life, open to settlers, were none too many and widely scattered. Perhaps half a dozen were found in a quarter century, and of that six maybe only one was suitable for human life without any costly and lengthy adaption of man or world. Warlock was one of the lucky finds which came so seldom.

Throgs were predators, living on the loot they garnered. As yet, mankind had not been able to discover whether they did indeed swarm from any home world.

2

Perhaps they lived eternally on board their plate ships with no permanent base, forced into a wandering life by the destruction of the planet on which they had originally been spawned. But they were raiders now, laying waste defenseless worlds, picking up the wealth of shattered cities in which no native life remained. And their hidden temporary bases were looped about the galaxy, their need for worlds with an atmosphere similar to Terra's as necessary as that of man. For in spite of their grotesque insectile bodies, their wholly alien minds, the Throgs were warm-blooded, oxygen-breathing creatures.

After the first few clashes the early Terran explorers had endeavored to promote a truce between the species, only to discover that between Throg and man there appeared to be no meeting ground at all—total difference of mental processes producing insurmountable misunderstanding. There was simply no point of communication. So the Terrans had suffered one smarting defeat after another until they perfected the grid. And now their colonies were safe, at least when time worked in their favor.

It had not on Warlock.

A last vivid lash of red cracked over the huddle of domes in the valley. Shann blinked, half blinded by that glare. His jaws ached as he unclenched his teeth. That was the finish. Breathing raggedly, he raised his head, beginning to realize that he was the only one of his kind left alive on a none-too-hospitable world controlled by enemies—without shelter or supplies.

He edged back into the narrow cleft which was the entrance to the ledge. As a representative of his species he was not impressive, and now with those shudders he could not master, shaking his thin body, he looked even smaller and more vulnerable. Shann drew his knees up close under his chin. The hood of his woodsman's jacket was pushed back in spite of the chill of the morning, and

3

he wiped the back of his hand across his lips and chin in an oddly childish gesture.

None of the men below who had been alive only minutes earlier had been close friends of his; Shann had never known anyone but acquaintances in his short, roving life. Most people had ignored him completely except to give orders, and one or two had been actively malicious—like Garth Thorvald. Shann grimaced at a certain recent memory, and then that grimace faded into wonder. If young Thorvald hadn't purposefully tried to get Shann into trouble by opening the wolverines' cage, Shann wouldn't be here now—alive and safe for a time— he'd have been down there with the others.

The wolverines! For the first time since Shann had heard the crackle of the Throg attack he remembered the reason he had been heading into the hills. Of all the men on the Survey team, Shann Lantee had been the least important. The dirty, tedious clean-up jobs, the dull routines which required no technical training but which had to be performed to keep the camp functioning comfortably, those had been his portion. And he had accepted that status willingly, just to have a chance to be included among Survey personnel. Not that he had the slightest hope of climbing up to even an S-E-Three rating in the service.

Part of those menial activities had been to clean the animal cages. And there Shann Lantee had found something new, something so absorbing that most of the tiring dull labor had ceased to exist except as tasks to finish before he could return to the fascination of the animal runs.

Survey teams had early discovered the advantage of using mutated and highly trained Terran animals as assistants in the exploration of strange worlds. From the biological laboratories and breeding farms on Terra came

4

trickle of specialized aides-de-camp to accompany man
to space. Some were fighters, silent, more deadly than
eapons a man wore at his belt or carried in his hands.
ome were keener eyes, keener noses, keener scouts than
e human kind could produce. Bred for intelligence, for
ze, for adaptability to alien conditions, the animal ex-
lorers from Terra were prized.

Wolverines, the ancient "devils" of the northlands on
erra, were being tried for the first time on Warlock.
heir caution, a quality highly developed in their breed,
ade them testers for new territory. Able to tackle in
attle an animal three times their size, they should be
dded protection for the man they accompanied into the
ilderness, and their wide ranging, their ability to climb
nd swim, and above all, their curiosity were assets.

Shann had begun contact by cleaning their cages; he
nded captivated by these miniature bears with long
ushy tails. And to his unbounded delight the attraction
as mutual. Alone to Taggi and Togi he was a person, an
nportant person. Those teeth, which could tear flesh
to ragged strips, nipped gently at his fingers, closed
ithout any pressure on arm, even on nose and chin in
hat was the ultimate caress of their kind. Since they
ere escape artists of no mean ability, twice he had had
track and lead them back to camp from forays of their
wn devising.

But the second time he had been caught by Fadakar,
e chief of animal control, before he could lock up the
elinquents. And the memory of the resulting interview
till had the power to make him flush with impotent
nger. Shann's explanation had been contemptuously
rushed aside, and he had been delivered an ultimatum.
f his carelessness occurred again, he would be sent back
n the next supply ship, to be dismissed without an offi-
ial sign-off on his work record, thus locked out of even

the lowest level of Survey for the rest of his life.

That was why Garth Thorvald's act of the night befor had made Shann brave the unknown darkness of Wa lock alone when he had discovered that the test anima were gone. He had to locate and return them befor Fadakar made his morning inspection; Garth Thorvald attempt to get him into bad trouble had saved his lif

Shann cowered back, striving to make his huddle body as small as possible. One of the Throg flyers ap peared silently out of the misty amber of the mornin sky, hovering over the silent camp. The aliens were com ing in to inspect the site of their victory. And the safe place for any Terran now was as far from the vicinity o those silent domes as he could get. Shann's slight bod was an asset as he wedged through the narrow mouth o a cleft and so back into the cliff wall. The climb befor him he knew in part, for this was the path the wolverine had followed on their two other escapes. A few moment of tricky scrambling and he was out in a cuplike depres sion choked with brush covered with the purplish foliag of Warlock. On the other side of that was a small cut to sloping hillside, giving on another valley, not as wide a that in which the camp stood, but one well provided wit cover in the way of trees and high-growing bushes.

A light wind pushed among the trees, and twice Shan heard the harsh, rasping call of a clak-clak—one of th batlike leather-winged flyers that laired in pits along th cliff walls. That present snap of two-tone complaint sug gested that the land was empty of strangers. For the clak claks vociferously and loudly resented encroachment o their chosen hunting territory.

Shann hesitated. He was driven by the urge to put a much distance between him and the landing Throg shi as he could. But to arouse the attention of inquisitiv clak-claks was asking for trouble. Perhaps it would b est to keep on along the top of the cliff, rather than risk descent to take cover in the valley the flyers patrolled.

A patch of dust, sheltered by a tooth-shaped projection f rock, gave the Terran his first proof that Taggi and his nate had preceded him, for printed firmly there was the amiliar paw mark of a wolverine. Shann began to hope hat both animals had taken to cover in the wilderness head.

He licked dry lips. Having left secretly without any mergency pack, he had no canteen, and now Shann inentoried his scant possessions—a field kit, heavy-duty lothing, a short hooded jacket with attached mittens, the reast marked with the Survey insignia. His belt supported a sheathed stunner and bush knife, and seam ockets held three credit tokens, a twist of wire intended o reinforce the latch of the wolverine cage, a packet of ravo tablets, two identity and work cards, and a length f cord. No rations—save the bravos—no extra charge for is stunner. But he did have, weighing down a loop on he jacket, a small atomic torch.

The path he followed ended abruptly in a cliff drop, nd Shann made a face at the odor rising from below, ven though that scent meant he could climb down to the alley floor here without fearing any clak-clak attention. Chemical fumes from a mineral spring funneled against he wall, warding off any nesting in this section.

Shann drew up the hood of his jacket and snapped the ransparent face mask into place. He must get away— hen find food, water, a hiding place. That will to live vhich had made Shann Lantree fight innumerable battles n the past was in command, bracing him with a stubborn determination.

The fumes swirled up in a smoke haze about his waist, out he strode on, heading for the open valley and cleaner air. That stickly lavender vegetation bordering the spring

7

deepened in color to the normal purple-green, and then he was in a grove of trees, their branches pointed sky ward at sharp angles to the rust-red trunks.

A small skitterer burst from moss-spotted ground cov ering, giving an alarmed squeak, skimming out of sight as suddenly as it had appeared. Shann squeezed between two trees and then paused. The trunk of the larger was deeply scored with scratches dripping viscid gobs of sap a sap which was a bright froth of scarlet. Taggi had left his mark here, and not too long ago.

The soft carpet of moss showed no paw marks, but he thought he knew the goal of the animals—a lake down valley. Shann was beginning to plan now. The Throgs had not blasted the Terran camp out of existence; they had only made sure of the death of its occupiers. Which meant they must have some use for the installations. For the general loot of a Survey field camp would be rela tively worthless to those who picked over the treasure of entire cities elsewhere. Why? What did the Throgs want? And would the alien invaders continue to occupy the domes for long?

Shann did not realize what had happened to him since that shock of ruthless attack. From early childhood, when he had been thrown on his own to scratch a living—a borderline existence of a living—on the Dumps of Tyr he had had to use his wits to keep life in a scrawny and undersized body. However, since he had been eating reg ularly from Survey rations, he was not quite so scrawny any more.

His formal education was close to zero, his informal and off-center schooling vast. And that particular tough ening process which had been working on him for years now aided in his speedy adaption to a new set of facts, formidable ones. He was alone on a strange and perhaps hostile world. Water, food, safe shelter, those were im-

8

portant now. And once again, away from the ordered round of the camp where he had been ruled by the desires and requirements of others, he was thinking, planning in freedom. Later (his hand went to the butt of his stunner) perhaps later he might just find a way of extracting an accounting from the beetle-faces, too.

For the present, he would have to keep away from the Throgs, which meant well away from the camp. A fleck of green showed through the amethyst foliage before him —the lake! Shann wriggled through a last bush barrier and stood to look out over that surface. A sleek brown head bobbed up. Shann put fingers to his mouth and whistled. The head turned, black button eyes regarded him, short legs began to churn water. To his gratification the swimmer was obeying his summons.

Taggi came ashore, pausing on the fine gray sand of the verge to shake himself vigorously. Then the wolverine came upslope at a clumsy gallop to Shann. With an unknown feeling swelling inside him the Terran went down on both knees, burying both hands in the coarse brown fur, warming to the uproarious welcome Taggi gave him.

"Togi?" Shann asked as if the other could answer. He gazed back to the lake, but Taggi's mate was nowhere in sight.

The blunt head under his hand swung around, black button nose pointed north. Shann had never been sure just how intelligent, as mankind measured intelligence, the wolverines were. He had come to suspect that Fadakar and the other experts had underrated them and that both beasts understood more than they were given credit for. Now he followed an experiment of his own, one he had had a chance to try only a few times before and never at length. Pressing his palm flat on Taggi's head, Shann thought of Throgs and of their attack, trying to arouse in the animal a corresponding reaction to his own horror and anger.

And Taggi responded. A mutter became a growl, teeth gleamed—those cruel teeth of a carnivore to whom they were weapons of aggression. Danger . . . Shann thought "danger." Then he raised his hand, and the wolverine shuffled off, heading north. The man followed.

They discovered Togi busy in a small cove where a jagged tangle of drift made a mat dating from the last high-water period. She was finishing a hearty breakfast, the remains of a water rat being buried thriftily against future need after the instincts of her kind. When she was done she came to Shann, inquiry plain to read in her eyes.

There was water here, and good hunting. But the site was too close to the Throgs. Let one of their exploring flyers sight them, and the little group was finished. Better cover, that's what the three fugitives must have. Shann scowled, not at Togi, but at the landscape. He was tired and hungry, but he must keep on going.

A stream fed into the cove from the west, a guide of sorts. With very little knowledge of the countryside, Shann was inclined to follow that.

Overhead the sun made its usual golden haze of the sky. A flight of vivid green streaks marked a flock of lake ducks coming for a morning feeding. Lake duck was good eating, but Shann had no time to hunt one now. Togi started down the bank of the stream, Taggi behind her. Either they had caught his choice subtly through some undefined mental contact, or they had already picked that road on their own.

Shann's attention was caught by a piece of the drift. He twisted the length free and had his first weapon of his own manufacture, a club. Using it to hold back a low sweeping branch, he followed the wolverines.

Within the half hour he had breakfast, too. A pair of limp skitterers, their long hind feet lashed together with a thong of grass, hung from his belt. They were not particularly good eating, but they were meat and acceptable.

The three, man and wolverines, made their way up the stream to the valley wall and through a feeder ravine into the larger space beyond. There, where the stream was born at the foot of a falls, they made their first camp. Judging that the morning haze would veil any smoke, Shann built a pocket-size fire. He seared rather than roasted the skitterers after he had made an awkward and messy business of skinning them, and tore the meat from the delicate bones in greedy mouthfuls. The wolverines lay side by side on the gravel, now and again raising a head alertly to test the scent on the air, or gaze into the distance.

Taggi made a warning sound deep in the throat. Shann tossed handfuls of sand over the dying fire. He had only time to fling himself face-down, hoping the drab and weathered cloth of his uniform faded into the color of the earth on which he lay, every muscle tense.

A shadow swung across the hillside. Shann's shoulders hunched, and he cowered again. That terror he had known on the ledge was back in full force as he waited for the beam to lick at him as it had earlier at his fellows. The Throgs were on the hunt. . . .

2. DEATH OF A SHIP

THAT sight of displaced air was not as loud as a breeze, but it echoed monstrously in Shann's ears. He could not believe in his luck as that sound grew fainter, drew away into the valley he had just left. With infinite caution he raised his head from his arm, still hardly able to accept the fact that he had not been sighted, that the Throgs and their flyer were gone.

But that black plate was spinning out into the sun haze. One of the beetles might have suspected that there were Terran fugitives and ordered a routine patrol. After all, how could the aliens know that they had caught all but one of the Survey party in camp? Though with all the Terran scout flitters grounded on the field, the men dead in their bunks, the surprise would seem to be complete.

As Shann moved, Taggi and Togi came to life also. They had gone to earth with speed, and the man was sure that both beasts had sensed danger. Not for the first time he knew a burning desire for the formal education he had never had. In camp he had listened, dragging out routine jobs in order to overhear reports and the small talk of specialists keen on their own particular hobbies. But so much of the information Shann had thus picked up to store in a retentive memory he had not understood and could not fit together. It had been as if he were trying to solve some highly important puzzle with at least a quarter of the necessary pieces missing, or with unrelated bits from others intermixed. How much control did a trained animal scout have over his furred or feathered assistants? And was part of that mastery a mental rapport built up between man and animal?

How well would the wolverines obey him now, especially when they would not return to camp where cages stood waiting as symbols of human authority? Wouldn't a trek into the wilderness bring about a revolt for complete freedom? If Shann could depend upon the animals, it would mean a great deal. Not only would their superior hunting ability provide all three with food, but their scouting senses, so much keener than his, might erect a slender wall between life and death.

Few large native beasts had been discovered on War-lock by the Terran explorers. And of those four or five different species, none had proved hostile if unprovoked. But that did not mean that somewhere back in the wild lands into which Shann was heading there were no here-tofore unknowns, perhaps slyer and as vicious as the wolverines when they were aroused to rage.

Then there were the "dreams," which had afforded the prime source of camp discussion and dispute. Shann brushed coarse sand from his boots and thought about the dreams. Did they or did they not exist? You could start an argument any time by making a definite state-ment for or against the peculiar sort of dreaming re-ported by the first scout to set ship on this world.

The Circe system, of which Warlock was the second of three planets, had first been scouted four years ago by one of those explorers traveling solo in Survey service. Everyone knew that the First-In Scouts were a weird breed, almost a mutation of Terran stock—their reports were rife with strange observations.

So an alarming one concerning Circe (a yellow sun such as Sol) and her three planets was not so rare. Witch, the world nearest in orbit to Circe, was too hot for human occupancy without drastic and too costly world-changing. Wizard, the third out from the sun, was mostly bare rock and highly poisonous water. But Warlock, swinging through space between two forbidding neigh-bors, seemed to be just what the settlement board or-dered.

Then the Survey scout, even in the cocoon safety of his well-armed ship, began to dream. And from those dreams a horror of the apparently empty world developed, until he fled the planet to preserve his sanity. There had been a second visit to Warlock in check; worlds so well adapted to human emigration could not be lightly thrown away. And this time there was a negative report, no trace of dreams, no registration of any outside influence on the delicate and complicated equipment the ship carried. So the Survey team had been dispatched to prepare for the coming of the first pioneers, and none of them had dreamed either—at least, no more than the ordinary dreams all men accepted.

Only there were those who pointed out that the seasons had changed between the first and second visits to Warlock. That first scout had planeted in summer; his successors had come in fall and winter. They argued that the final release of world for settlement should not be given until the full year on Warlock had been sampled.

But the pressure of Emigrant Control had forced their hands, that and the fear of just what had eventually happened—an attack from the Throgs. So they had speeded up the process of declaring Warlock open. Only Ragnar Thorvald had protested that decision up to the last and had gone back to headquarters on the supply ship a month ago to make a last appeal for a more careful study.

Shann stopped brushing the sand from the tough fabric above his knee. Ragnar Thorvald . . . He remembered back to the port landing apron on another world, remembered with a sense of loss he could not define. That had been about the second biggest day of his short life; the biggest had come earlier when they had actually allowed him to sign on for Survey duty. .

He had tumbled off the cross-continent cargo carrier, his kit—a very meager kit—slung over his thin shoulder, a hot eagerness expanding inside him until he thought that he could not continue to throttle down that wild happiness. There was a waiting starship. And he—Shann Lantee from the Dumps of Tyr, without any influence or schooling—was going to blast off in her, wearing the

14

brown-green uniform of Survey!

Then he had hesitated uncertainly, had not quite dared cross the few feet of apron lying between him and that compact group wearing the same uniform—with a slight difference, that of service bars and completion badges and rank insignia—with the unconscious self-assurance of men who had done this many times before.

But after a moment that whole group had become in his own shy appraisal just a background for one man. Shann had never before known in his pinched and limited childhood, his lost boyhood, anyone who aroused in him hero worship. And he could not have put a name to the new emotion that added so suddenly to his burning desire to make good, not only to hold the small niche in Survey which he had already so painfully achieved, but to climb, until he could stand so in such a group talking easily to that tall man, his uncovered head bronze-yellow in the sunlight, his cool gray eyes pale in his brown face.

Not that any of those wild dreams born in that minute or two had been realized in the ensuing months. Probably those dreams had always been as wild as the ones reported by the first scout on Warlock. Shann grinned wryly now at the short period of childish hope and half-confidence that he could do big things. Only one Thorvald had ever noticed Shann's existence in the Survey camp, and that had been Garth.

Garth Thorvald, a far less impressive—one could say "smudged"—copy of his brother. Swaggering with an arrogance Ragnar never showed, Garth was a cadet on his first mission, intent upon making Shann realize the unbridgeable gulf between a labor hand and an officer-to-be. He had appeared to know right from their first meeting just how to make Shann's life a misery.

Now, in this slit of valley wall away from the domes, Shann's fists balled. He pounded them against the earth in a way he had so often hoped to plant them on Garth's smoothly handsome face, his well-muscled body. One didn't survive the Dumps of Tyr without learning how to use fists, and boots, and a list of tricks they didn't teach in any academy. He had always been sure that he could take Garth if they mixed it up. But if he had loosed the tight rein he had kept on his temper and offered that challenge, he would have lost his chance with Survey. Garth had proved himself able to talk his way out of any scrape, even minor derelictions of duty, and he far outranked Shann. The laborer from Tyr had had to swallow all that the other could dish out and hope that on his next assignment he would not be a member of young Thorvald's team. Though, because of Garth Thorvald, Shann's toll of black record marks had mounted dangerously high and each day the chance for any more duty tours had grown dimmer.

Shann laughed, and the sound was ugly. That was one thing he didn't have to worry about any longer. There would be no other assignments for him, the Throgs had seen to that. And Garth . . . well, there would never be a showdown between them now. He stood up. The Throg ship had disappeared; they could push on.

He found a break in the cliff wall which was climbable, and he coaxed the wolverines after him. When they stood on the heights from which the falls tumbled, Taggi and Togi rubbed against him, cried for his attention. They, too, appeared to need the reassurance they got from contact with him, for they were also fugitives on this alien world, the only representatives of their kind.

Since he did not have any definite goal in view, Shann continued to be guided by the stream, following its wanderings across a plateau. The sun was warm, so he carried his jacket slung across one shoulder. Taggi and Togi ranged ahead, twice catching skitterers, which they devoured voraciously. A shadow on a sun-baked rock sent the Terran skidding for cover until he saw that it was cast by one of the questing falcons from the upper peaks. But that shook his confidence, so he again sought cover, ashamed at his own carelessness.

In the late afternoon he reached the far end of the plateau, faced a climb to peaks which still bore cones of snow, now tinted a soft peach by the sun. Shann studied that possible path and distrusted his own powers to take it without proper equipment or supplies. He must turn either north or south, though he would then have to abandon a sure water supply in the stream. Tonight he would camp where he was. He had not realized how tired he was until he found a likely half-cave in the mountain wall and crawled in. There was too much danger in fire here; he would have to do without that first comfort of his kind.

Luckily, the wolverines squeezed in beside him to fill the hole. With their warm furred bodies sandwiching him, Shann dozed, awoke, and dozed again, listening to night sounds—the screams, cries, hunting calls, of the Warlock wilds. Now and again one of the wolverines whined and moved uneasily.

Fingers of sun picked at Shann through a shaft among the rocks, striking his eyes. He moved, blinked blearily awake, unable for the first few seconds to understand why the smooth plasta wall of his bunk had become rough red stone. Then he remembered. He was alone and he threw himself frantically out of the cave, afraid the wolverines had wandered off. Only both animals were busy clawing under a boulder with a steady persistence which argued there was a purpose behind that effort.

A sharp sting on the back of one hand made that purpose only too clear to Shann, and he retreated hurriedly from the vicinity of the excavation. They had found an earth-wasp's burrow and were hunting grubs, naturally arousing the rightful inhabitants to bitter resentment.

Shann faced the problem of his own breakfast. He had had the immunity shots given to all members of the team, and he had eaten game brought in by exploring parties and labeled "safe." But how long he could keep to the varieties of native food he knew was uncertain. Sooner or later he must experiment for himself. Already he drank the stream water without the aid of purifiers, and so far there had been no ill results from that necessary reckless-ness. Now the stream suggested fish. But instead he chanced upon another water inhabitant which had crawled up on land for some obscure purpose of its own. It was a sluggish scaled thing, an easy victim to his club, with thin, weak legs it could project at will from a finned and armor-plated body.

Shann offered the head and guts to Togi, who had abandoned the wasp nest. She sniffed in careful investi-gation and then gulped. Shann built a small fire and seared the firm greenish flesh. The taste was flat, lacking salt, but the food eased his emptiness. Enheartened, he started south, hoping to find water sometime during the morning.

By noon he had his optimism justified with the dis-covery of a spring, and the wolverines had brought down a slender-legged animal whose coat was close in shade to the dusky purple of the vegetation. Smaller than a Terran deer, its head bore, not horns, but a ridge of stiffened hair rising in a point some twelve inches about the skull dome. Shann haggled off some ragged steaks while the wolverines feasted in earnest, carefully burying the head afterward.

It was when Shann knelt by the spring pool to wash that he caught the clamor of the clak-claks. He had seen or heard nothing of the flyers since he had left the lake valley. But from the noise now rising in an earsplitting volume, he thought there was a a sizable colony near-by and that the inhabitants were thoroughly aroused.

He crept on his hands and knees to near-by brush cover, heading toward the source of that outburst. If the claks were announcing a Throg scouting party, he wanted to know it.

Lying flat, with branches forming a screen over him, the Terran gazed out on a stretch of grassland which sloped at a fairly steep angle to the south and which must lead to a portion of countryside well below the level he was now traversing.

The clak-claks were skimming back and forth, shrieking their staccato war cries. Following the erratic dashes of their flight formation, Shann decided that whatever they railed against was on the lower level, out of his sight from that point. Should he simply withdraw, since the disturbance was not near him? Prudence dictated that; yet still he hesitated.

He had no desire to travel north, or to try and scale the mountains. No, south was his best path, and he should be very sure that route was closed before he retreated.

Since any additional fuss the clak-claks might make on sighting him would be undistinguished in their now general clamor, the Terran crawled on to where tall grass provided a screen at the top of the slope. There he stopped short, his hands digging into the earth in sudden braking action.

Below, the ground steamed from a rocket flare-back, grasses burned away from the fins of a small scoutship. But even as Shann rose to one knee, his shout of welcome choked in his throat. One of those fins sank, canting the ship crookedly, preventing any new take-off. And over the crown of a low hill to the west swung the ominous black plate of a Throg flyer.

The Throg ship came up in a burst of speed, and Shann waited tensely for some countermove from the scout. Those small speedy Terran ships were prudently provided with weapons triply deadly in proportion to their size. He was sure that the Terran ship could hold its own against the Throg, even eliminate the enemy. But there was no fire from the slanting pencil of the scout. The Throg circled warily, obviously expecting a trap. Twice it darted back in the direction from which it had come. As it returned from its second retreat, another of its kind showed, a black coin dot against the amber of the sky.

Shann felt sick inside. Now the Terran scout had lost any advantage and perhaps all hope. The Throgs could box the other in, cut the downed ship to pieces with their energy beams. He wanted to crawl away and not witness this last disaster for his kind. But some stubborn core of will kept him where he was.

The Throgs began to circle while beneath them the flock of clak-claks screamed and dived at the slanting nose of the Terran ship. Then that same slashing energy he had watched quarter the camp snapped from the far plate across the stricken scout. The man who had piloted her, if not dead already (which might account for the lack of defense), must have fallen victim to that. But the Throg was going to make very sure. The second flyer halted, remaining poised long enough to unleash a second bolt—dazzling any watching eyes and broadcasting a vibration to make Shann's skin crawl when the last faint ripple reached his lookout post.

What happened then the overconfident Throg was not prepared to take. Shann cried out, burying his face on his arm, as pinwheels of scarlet light blotted out normal sight. There was an explosion, a deafening blast. He cowered, blind, unable to hear. Then, rubbing at his eyes, he tried to see what had happened.

Through watery blurs he made out the Throg ship, not swinging now in serene indifference to Warlock's gravity, but whirling end over end across the sky as might a leaf tossed in a gust of wind. Its rim caught against a rust-red cliff, it rebounded and crumpled. Then it came down, smashing perhaps half a mile away from the smoking crater in which lay the mangled wreckage of the Terran ship. The disabled scout pilot must have played a last desperate game, making of his ship bait for a trap.

The Terran had taken one Throg with him. Shann rubbed again at his eyes, just barely able to catch a glimpse of the second ship flashing away westward. Perhaps it was only his impaired sight, but it appeared to him that the Throg followed an erratic path, either as if the pilot feared to be caught by a second shot, or because that ship had also suffered some injury.

Acid smoke wreathed up from the valley making Shann retch and cough. There could be no survivor from the Terran scout, and he did not believe that any Throg had lived to crawl free of the crumpled plate. But there would be other beetles swarming here soon. They would not dare to leave the scene unsearched. He wondered about that scout. Had the pilot been aiming for the Survey camp, the absence of any rider beam from there warning him off so that he made the detour which brought him here? Or had the Throgs tried to blast the Terran ship in the upper atmosphere, crippling it, making this a forced landing? But at least this battle had cost the Throgs, settling a small portion of the Terran debt for the lost camp.

The length of time between Shann's sighting of the grounded ship and the attack by the Throgs had been so short that he had not really developed any strong hope of rescue to be destroyed by the end of the crippled ship. On the other hand, seeing the Throgs take a beating had exploded his subconscious acceptance of their superiority. He might not have even the resources of a damaged scout at his command. But he did have Taggi, Togi, and his own brain. Since he was fated to permanent exile on Warlock, there might just be some way to make the beetles pay for that.

He licked his lips. Real action against the aliens would take a lot of planning. Shann would have to know more about what made a Throg a Throg, more than all the wild stories he had heard over the years. There *had* to be some way a Terran could move effectively against a beetle-head. And he had a lot of time, maybe the rest of his life to work out a few answers. That Throg ship lying wrecked at the foot of the cliff . . . perhaps he could do a little investigating before any rescue squad arrived. Shann decided such a move was worth the try and whistled to the wolverines.

3. TO CLOSE RANKS

SHANN made his way at an angle to avoid the smoking pit cradling the wreckage of the Terran ship. There were no signs of life about the Throg plate as he approached. A quarter of its bulk was telescoped back into the rest, and surely none of the aliens could have survived such a smash, tough as they were reputed to be with those horny carapaces serving them in place of more vulnerable human skin.

He sniffed. There was a nauseous odor heavy on the

morning air, one which would make a lasting impression on any human nose. The port door in the black ship stood open, perhaps having burst in the impact against the cliff. Shann had almost reached it when a crackle of chain lightning beat across the ground before him, turning the edge of the buckled entrance panel red.

Shann dropped to the ground, drawing his stunner, knowing at the same moment that such a weapon was about as much use in meeting a blaster as a straw wand would be to ward off a blazing coal. A chill numbness held him as he waited for a second blast to char the flesh between his shoulders. So there had been a Throg survivor, after all.

But as moments passed and the Throg did not move in to make an easy kill, Shann collected his wits. Only one shot! Was the beetle injured, unable to make sure of even an almost defenseless prey? The Throgs seldom took prisoners. When they did . . .

The Terran's lips tightened. He worked his hand under his prone body, feeling for the hilt of his knife. With that he could speedily remove himself from the status of Throg prisoner, and he would do it gladly if there was no hope of escape. Had there been only one charge left in that blaster? Shann could make half a dozen guesses as to why the other had made no move, but that shot had come from behind him, and he darcd not turn his head or otherwise make an effort to see what the other might be doing.

Was it only his imagination, or had that stench grown stronger during the last few seconds? Could the Throg be creeping up on him? Shann strained his ears, trying to catch some sound he could interpret. The few clak-claks that had survived the blast about the ship were shrieking overhead, and Shann made one attempt at counterattack.

He whistled the wolverines' call. The pair had been too

23

willing to follow him down into this valley, and they had avoided the crater at a very wide circle. But if they would obey him now, he just might have a chance.

There! That *had* been a sound, and the smell *was* stronger. The Throg must be coming to him. Again Shann whistled, holding in his mind his hatred for the beetlehead, the need for finishing off that alien. If the animals could pick either thoughts or emotions out of their human companion, this was the time for him to get those unspoken half-orders across.

Shann slammed his hand hard against the ground, sent his body rolling, his stunner up and ready.

And now he could see that grotesque thing, swaying weakly back and forth on its thin legs, yet holding a blaster, bringing that weapon up to center it on him. The Throg was hunched over and perhaps to Taggi presented the outline of some four-footed creature to be hunted. For the wolverine male sprang for the horn-shelled shoulders.

Under that impact that Throg sagged forward. But Taggi, outraged at the nature of creature he had attacked, squalled and retreated. Shann had had his precious seconds of distraction. He fired, the core of the stun beam striking full into the flat dish of the alien's "face."

That bolt, which would have shocked a mammal into insensibility, only slowed the Throg. Shann rolled again, gaining a temporary cover behind the wrecked ship. He squirmed under metal hot enough to scorch his jacket and saw the reflection of a second blaster shot which had been fired seconds late.

Now the Throg had him tied down. But to get at the Terran the alien would have to show himself, and Shann had one chance in fifty, which was better than that of three minutes ago—when the odds had been set at one in a hundred. He knew that he could not press the wolverines in again. Taggi's distaste was too manifest; Shann had been lucky that the animal had made one abortive attack.

Perhaps the Terran's escape and Taggi's action had made the alien reckless. Shann had no clue to the thinking processes of the non-human but now the Throg staggered around the end of the plate, his digits, which were closer to claws than fingers, fumbling with his weapon. The Terran snapped another shot from his stunner, hoping to slow the enemy down. But he was trapped. If he turned to climb the cliff at his back, the beetle-head could easily pick him off.

A rock hurtled from the heights above, striking with deadly accuracy on the domed, hairless head of the Throg. His armored body crashed forward, struck against the ship, and rebounded to the ground. Shann darted forward to seize the blaster, kicking loose the claws which still grasped it, before he flattened back to the cliff, the strange weapon over his arm, his heart beating wildly.

That rock had not bounded down the mountainside by chance; it had been hurled with intent and aimed carefully at its target. And no Throg would kill one of his fellows. Or would he? Suppose orders had been issued to take a Terran prisoner and the Throg by the ship had disobeyed? Then, why a rock and not a blaster bolt?

Shann edged along until the upslanted, broken side of the Throg flyer provided him with protection from any overhead attack. Under that shelter he waited for the next move from his unknown rescuer.

The clak-claks wheeled closer to earth. One lit boldly on the carapace of the inert Throg, shuffling ungainly along that horny ridge. Cradling the blaster, the Terran continued to wait. His patience was rewarded when that investigating clak-clak took off uttering an enraged snap or two. He heard what might be the scrape of boots across rock, but that might also have come from horny skin meeting stone.

Then the other must have lost his footing not too far above. Accompanied by a miniature landslide of stones and earth, a figure slid down several yards away. Shann waited in a half-crouch, his looted blaster covering the man now getting to his feet. There was no mistaking the familiar uniform, or even the man. How Ragnar Thorvald had reached that particular spot on Warlock or why, Shann could not know. But that he was there, there was no denying.

Shann hurried forward. It had been when he caught his first sight of Thorvald that he realized just how deep his unacknowledged loneliness had bit. There were two Terrans on Warlock now, and he did not need to know why. But Thorvald was staring back at him with the blankness of non-recognition.

"Who are you?" The demand held something close to suspicion.

That note in the other's voice wiped away a measure of Shann's confidence, threatened something which had flowered in him since he had struck into the wilderness on his own. Three words had reduced him again to Lantee, unskilled laborer.

"Lantee. I'm from the camp ..."

Thorvald's eagerness was plain in his next question: "How many of you got away? Where are the rest?" He gazed past Shann up the plateau slope as if he expected to see the personnel of the camp sprout out of the cloak of grass along the verge.

"Just me and the wolverines," Shann answered in a colorless voice. He cradled the blaster on his hip, turned a little away from the officer.

"You . . . and the wolverines?" Thorvald was plainly startled. "But . . . where? How?"

"The Throgs hit very early yesterday morning. They caught the rest in camp. The wolverines had escaped from their cage, and I was out hunting them . . ." He told his story baldly.

"You're sure about the rest?" Thorvald had a thin steel of rage edging his voice. Almost, Shann thought, as if he could turn that blade of rage against one Shann Lantee for being yet alive when more important men had not survived.

"I saw the attack from an upper ridge," the younger man said, having been put on the defensive. Yet he had a right to be alive, hadn't he? Or did Thorvald believe that he should have gone running down to meet the beetle-heads with his useless stunner? "They used energy beams . . . didn't land until it was all over."

"I knew there was something wrong when the camp didn't answer our enter-atmosphere signal," Thorvald said absently. "Then one of those platters jumped us on braking orbit, and my pilot was killed. When we set down on the automatics here I had just time to rig a surprise for any trackers before I took to the hills—"

"The blast got one of them," Shann pointed out.

"Yes, they'd nicked the booster rocket; she wouldn't climb again. But they'll be back here to pick over the remains."

Shann looked at the dead Throg. "Thanks for taking a hand." His tone was as chill as the other's this time. "I'm heading south . . ."

And, he added silently, I intend to keep on that way. The Throg attack had dissolved the pattern of the Survey team. He didn't owe Thorvald any allegiance. And he had been successfully on his own here since the camp had been overrun.

"South," Thorvald repeated. "Well, that's as good a direction as any right now."

But they were not united. Shann found the wolverines and patiently coaxed and wheedled them into coming with him over a circuitous route which kept them away from both ships. Thorvald went up the cliff, swung down again, a supply bag slung over one shoulder. He stood watching as Shann brought the animals in.

Then Thorvald's arm swept out, his fingers closing possessively about the barrel of the blaster. Shann's own hold on the weapon tightened, and the force of the other's pull dragged him partly around.

"Let's have that—"

"Why?" Shann supposed that because it had been the other's well-aimed rock which had put the Throg out of commission permanently, the officer was going to claim their only spoils of war as personal booty, and a hot resentment flowered in the younger man.

"We don't take that away from here." Thorvald made the weapon his with a quick twist.

To Shann's utter astonishment, the Survey officer walked back to kneel beside the dead Throg. He worked the grip of the blaster under the alien's lax claws and inspected the result with the care of one arranging a special and highly important display. Shann's protest became vocal. "We'll need that!"

"It'll do us far more good right where it is . . ." Thorvald paused and then added, with impatience roughening his voice as if he disliked the need for making any explanations, "There is no reason for us to advertise our being alive. If the Throgs found a blaster missing, they'd start thinking and looking around. I want to have a breathing spell before I have to play quarry in one of their hunts."

Put that way, his action did make sense. But Shann

28

egretted the loss of an arm so superior to their own
veapons. Now they could not loot the plateship either. In
ilence he turned and started to trudge southward, with-
ut waiting for Thorvald to catch up with him.

Once away from the blasted area, the wolverines
anged ahead at their clumsy gallop, which covered
ground at a surprising rate of speed. Shann knew that
heir curiosity made them scouts surpassing any human
and that the men who followed would have ample warning of any danger to come. Without reference to his silent
rail companion, he sent the animals toward another strip
of woodland which would give them cover against the
coming of any Throg flyer.

As the hours advanced he began to cast about for a
proper night camp. The woods ought to give them a
usable site.

"This is a water wood," Thorvald said, breaking the
silence for the first time since they had left the wrecks.

Shann knew that the other had knowledge, not only of
he general countryside, but of exploring techniques
which he himself did not possess, but to be reminded of
that fact was an irritant rather than a reassurance. Without answering, the younger man bored on to locate the
water promised.

The wolverines found the small lake first and were
splashing along its shore when the Terrans caught up.
Thorvald went to work, but to Shann's surprise he did
not unstrap the forceblade ax at his belt. Bending over a
sapling, he pounded away with a stone at the green wood
a few inches above the root line until he was able to
break through the slender trunk. Shann drew his own
knife and bent to tackle another treelet when Thorvald
stopped him with an order: "Use a stone on that, the way
I did."

Shann could see no reason for such a laborious process.

If Thorvald did not want to use his ax, that was no rea son that Shann could not put his heavy belt knife to work. He hesitated, ready to set the blade to the outer bark of the tree.

"Look—" again that impatient edge in the officer's tone, the need for explanation seeming to come very hard to the other—"sooner or later, the Throgs might just trace us here and find this camp. If so, they are *not* going to discover any traces to label us Terran—"

"But who else could we be?" protested Shann. "There is no native race on Warlock."

Thorvald tossed his improvised stone ax from hand to hand.

"But do the Throgs know that?"

The implications, the possibilities, in that idea struck home to Shann. Now he began to understand what Thorvald might be planning.

"Now there *is* going to be a native race." Shann made that a statement instead of a question and saw that the other was watching him with a new intentness, as if he had at last been recognized as a person instead of rank and file and very low rank at that—Survey personnel.

"There is going to be a native race," Thorvald affirmed.

Shann resheathed his knife and went to search the pond beach for a suitable stone to use in its place. Even so, he made harder work of the clumsy chopping than Thorvald had. He worried at one sapling after another until his hands were skinned and his breath came in painful gusts from under aching ribs. Thorvald had gone on to another task, ripping the end of a long tough vine from just under the powdery surface of the thick leaf masses fallen in other years.

With this the officer lashed together the tops of the poles, having planted their splintered butts in the

30

round, so that he achieved a crudely conical erection.
Leafy branches were woven back and forth through this
framework, with an entrance, through which one might
crawl on hands and knees, left facing the lakeside. The
shelter they completed was compact and efficient but to-
ally unlike anything Shann had ever seen before, certainly far removed from the domes of the camp. He said
o, nursing his raw hands.

"An old form," Thorvald replied, "native to a primitive
ace on Terra. Certainly the beetle-heads haven't come
cross its like before."

"Are we going to stay here? Otherwise it is pretty
eavy work for one night's lodging."

Thorvald tested the shelter with a sharp shake. The
matted leaves whispered, but the framework held.

"Stage dressing. No, we won't linger here. But it's evi-
lence to support our play. Even a Throg isn't dense
nough to belive that natives would make a cross-country
rip without leaving evidence of their passing."

Shann sat down with a sigh he made no effort to sup-
press. He had a vision of Thorvald traveling southward,
methodically erecting these huts here and there to con-
ound Throgs who might not ever chance upon them. But
lready the Survey officer was busy with a new problem.

"We need weapons—"

"We have our stunners, a force ax, and our knives,"
Shann pointed out. He did not add, as he would have
iked that they could have had a blaster.

"Native weapons," Thorvald countered with his usual
nap. He went back to the beach and crawled about
here, choosing and rejecting stones picked out of the
gravel.

Shann scooped out a small pit just before their hut and
et about the making of a pocket-sized fire. He was hun-

31

gry and looked longingly now and again to the supply
bag Thorvald had brought with him. Dared he rummage
in that for rations? Surely the other would be carrying
concentrates.

"Who taught you how to make a fire that way?" Thorvald was back from the pond, a selection of round stones
about the size of his fist-resting between his chest and his
forearm.

"It's regulation, isn't it?" Shann countered defensively.

"It's regulation," Thorvald agreed. He set down his
stones in a row and then tossed the supply bag over to his
companion. "Too late to hunt tonight. But we'll have to
go easy on those rations until we can get more."

"Where?" Did Thorvald know of some supply cache
they could raid?

"From the Throgs," the other answered matter of
factly.

"But they don't eat our kind of food . . ."

"All the more reason for them to leave the camp supplies untouched."

"The camp?"

For the first time Thorvald's lips curved in a shadow
smile which was neither joyous nor warming. "A native
raid on an invaders' camp. What could be more natural?
And we'd better make it soon."

"But how can we?" To Shann what the other proposed
was sheer madness.

"There was once an ancient service corps on Terra,"
Thorvald answered, "which had a motto something like
this: 'The improbable we do at once; the impossible takes
a little longer.' What did you think we were going to do?
Sulk around out here in the bush and let the Throgs
claim Warlock for one of their pirate bases without opposition?"

Since that was the only future Shann had visualized, he was ready enough to admit the truth, only some shade of tone in the officer's voice kept him from saying so aloud.

4. SORTIE

FIVE days later they came up from the south so that this time Shann's view of the Terran camp was from a different angle. At first sight there had been little change in the general scene. He wondered if the aliens were using the Terran dome shelters themselves. Even in the twilight it was easy to pick out such landmarks as the com dome with the shaft of a broadcaster spearing from its top and the greater bulk of the supply warehouse.

"Two of their small flyers down on the landing field . . ." Thorvald materialized from the shadow, his voice a thread of whisper.

By Shann's side the wolverines were moving restlessly. Since Taggi's attack on the Throg neither beast would venture near any site where they could scent the aliens. This was the nearest point to which the men could urge either animal, which was a disappointment, for the wolverines would have been an excellent addition to the surprise sortie they planned for tonight, halving the danger for the men.

Shann ran his fingers across the coarse fur on the animals' shoulders, exerting a light pressure to signal them to wait. But he was not sure of their obedience. The foray was a crazy idea, and Shann wondered again why he had agreed to it. Yet he had gone along with Thorvald, even suggested a few modifications and additions of his own, such as the contents of the crude leaf sack now resting between his knees.

Thorvald flitted away, seeking his own post to the west. Shann was still waiting for the other's signal when there arose from the camp a sound to chill the flesh of any listener, a wail which could not have come from the throat of any normal living thing, intelligent being or animal. Ululating in eartorturing intensity, the cry sank to a faint, ominous echo of itself, to waver up the scale again.

The wolverines went mad. Shann had witnessed their quick kills in the wilds, but this stark ferocity of spitting, howling rage was new. They answered that challenge from the camp, streaking out from under his hands. Yet both animals skidded to a stop before they passed the first dome and were lost in the gloom. A spark glowed for an instant to his right; Thorvald was ready to go, so Shann had no time to try and recall the animals.

He fumbled for those balls of soaked moss in his leaf bag. The chemical smell from them blotted out that alien mustiness which the wind brought from the campsite. Shann readied the first sopping mess in his sling, snapped his fire sparker at it, and had the ball awhirl for a toss almost in one continuous movement. The moss burst into fire as it curved out and fell.

To a witness it might have seemed that the missile materialized out of the air, the effect being better than Shann had hoped.

A second ball for the sling—spark . . . out . . . down. The first had smashed on the ground near the dome of the com station, the force of impact flattening it into a round splatter of now fiercely burning material. And his second, carefully aimed, lit two feet beyond.

Another wail tearing at the nerves. Shann made a third

34

throw, a fourth. He had an audience now. In the light of those pools of fire the Throgs were scuttling back and forth, their hunched bodies casting weird shadows on the dome walls. They were making efforts to douse the fires, but Shann knew from careful experimentation that once ignited the stuff he had skimmed from the lip of one of the hot springs would go on burning as long as a fraction of its viscid substance remained unconsumed.

Now Thorvald had gone into action. A Throg suddenly halted, struggled frantically, and toppled over into the edge of a fire splotch, legs looped together by the coils of the curious weapon Thorvald had put together on their first night of partnership. Three round stones of comparable weight had each been fastened at the end of a vine cord, and those cords united at a center point. Thorvald had demonstrated the effectiveness of his creation by bringing down one of the small "deer" of the grasslands, an animal normally fleet enough to feel safe from both human and animal pursuit. And those weighted ropes now trapped the Throg with the same efficiency.

Having shot his last fireball, Shann ran swiftly to take up a new position, downgrade and to the east of the domes. Here he put into action another of the primitive weapons Thorvald had devised, a spear hurled with a throwing stick, giving it double range and twice as forceful penetration power. The spears themselves were hardly more than crudely shaped lengths of wood, their points charred in the fire. Perhaps these missiles could neither kill nor seriously wound. But more than one thudded home in a satisfactory fashion against the curving back carapace or the softer front parts of a Throg in a manner which certainly shook up and bruised the target. And one of Shann's victims went to the ground, to lie kicking in a way which suggested he had been more than just bruised.

Fireballs, spears . . . Thorvald had moved too. And now down into the somewhat frantic melee of the aroused camp fell a shower of slim weighted reeds, each provided with a clay-ball head. The majority of those balls broke on landing as the Terrans had intended. So, through the beetle smell of the aliens, spread the acrid, throat-parching fumes of the hot spring water. Whether those fumes had the same effect upon Throg breathing apparatus as they did upon Terran, the attackers could not tell, but they hoped such a bombardment would add to the general confusion.

Shann began to space the hurling of his crude spears with more care, trying to place them with all the precision of aim he could muster. There was a limit to their amount of varied ammunition, although they had dedicated every waking moment of the past few days to manufacture and testing. Luckily the enemy had had none of their energy beams at the domes. And so far they had made no move to lift their flyers for retaliation blasts.

But the Throgs were pulling themselves into order. Blaster fire cut the dusk. Most of the aliens were now flat on the ground, sending a creeping line of fire into the perimeter of the camp area. A dark form moved between Shann and the nearest patch of burning moss. The Terran raised a spear to the ready before he caught a whiff of the pungent scent emitted by a wolverine hot with battle rage. He whistled coaxingly. With the Throgs eager to blast any moving thing, the animals were in danger if they prowled about the scene.

That blunt head moved. Shann caught the glint of eyes in a furred mask; it was either Taggi or his mate. Then a puff of mixed Throg and chemical scent from the camp must have reached the wolverine. The animal coughed and fled westward, passing Shann.

Had Thorvald had time and opportunity to make his

planned raid on the supply dome? Time during such an embroilment was hard to measure, and Shann could not be sure. He began to count aloud, slowly, as they had agreed. When he reached one hundred he would begin his retreat; on two hundred he was to run for it, his goal the river a half mile from the camp.

The stream would take the fugitives to the sea where fiords cut the coastline into a ragged fringe offering a wealth of hiding places. Throgs seldom explored any territory on foot. For them to venture into that maze would be putting themselves at the mercy of the Terrans they hunted. And their flyers could comb the air above such a rocky wilderness without result.

Shann reached the count of one hundred. Twice a blaster bolt singed ground within distance close enough to make him wince, but most of the fire carried well above his head. All of his spears were gone, save for one he had kept, hoping for a last good target. One of the Throgs who appeared to be directing the fire of the others was facing Shann's position. And on pure chance that he might knock out that leader, Shann chose him for his victim.

The Terran had no illusions concerning his own marksmanship. The most he could hope for, he thought, was to have the primitive weapon thud home painfully on the other's armored hide. Perhaps, if he were very lucky, he could knock the other from his clawed feet. But that chance which hovers over any battlefield turned in Shann's favor. At just the right moment the Throg stretched his head up from the usual hunched position where the carapace extended over his wide shoulders to protect one of the alien's few vulnerable spots, the soft underside of his throat. And the fire-sharpened point of the spear went deep.

Throgs were mute, or at least none of them had ever

uttered a vocal sound to be reported by Terrans. This one did not cry out. But he staggered forward, forelimbs up, clawed digits pulling at the wooden pin transfixing his throat just under the mandible-equipped jaw, holding his head at an unnatural angle. Without seeming to notice the others of his kind, the Throg came on at a shambling run, straight at Shann as if he could actually see through the dark and had marked down the Terran for personal vengeance. There was something so uncanny about that forward dash that Shann retreated. As his hand groped for the knife at his belt his boot heel caught in a tangle of weed and he struggled for balance. The wounded Throg, still pulling at the spear shaft protruding above the swelling barrel of his chest, pounded on.

Shann sprawled backward and was caught in the elastic embrace of a bush, so he did not strike the ground. He fought the grip of prickly branches and kicked to gain solid earth under his feet. Then again he heard that piercing wail from the camp, as chilling as it had been the first time. Spurred by that, he won free. But he could not turn his back on the wounded Throg, keeping rather a sidewise retreat.

Already the alien had reached the dark beyond the rim of the camp. His progress now was marked by the crashing through low brush. Two of the Throgs back on the firing line started up after their leader. Shann caught a whiff of their odor as the wounded alien advanced with the single-mindedness of a robot.

It would be best to head for the river. Tall grass twisted about the Terran's legs as he began to run. In spite of the gloom, he hesitated to cross that open space. At night Warlock's peculiar vegetation displayed a very alien attribute—ten . . . twenty varieties of grass, plant, and tree emitted a wan phosphorescence, varying in degree, but affording each an aura of light. And the path before Shann now was dotted by splotches of that radiance, not as brilliant as the chemical-born flames the attackers had kindled in the camp, but as quick to betray the unwary who passed within their dim circles. And there had never been any reason to believe that Throg powers of sight were less than human; there was perhaps some evidence to the contrary. Shann crouched, charting the clumps ahead for a zigzag course which would take him to at least momentary safety in the river bed.

Perhaps a mile downstream was the transport the Terrans had cobbled together no earlier than this afternoon, a raft Thorvald had professed to believe would support them to the sea which lay some fifty Terran miles to the west. But now he had to cover that mile.

The wolverines? Thorvald? There was one lure which might draw the animals on to the rendezvous. Taggi had brought down a "deer" just before they had left the raft. And instead of allowing both beasts to feast at leisure, Shann had lashed the carcass to the shaky platform of wood and brush, putting it out to swing in the current, though still moored to the bank.

Wolverines always cached that part of the kill which they did not consume at the first eating, usually burying it. He had hoped that to leave the carcass in such a way would draw both animals back to the raft when they were hungry. And they had not fed particularly well that day.

Thorvald? Well, the Survey officer had made it very plain during the past five days of what Shann had come to look upon as an uneasy partnership that he considered himself far abler to manage in the field, while he had grave doubts of Shann's efficiency in the direction of survival potential.

The Terran started along the pattern of retreat he had laid out to the river bed. His heart pounded as he ran, not because of the physical effort he was expending, but because again from the camp had come that blood-freezing howl. A lighter line marked the lip of the cut in which the stream was set, something he had not foreseen. He threw himself down to crawl the last few feet, hugging the earth.

That very pale luminescence was easily accounted for by what lay below. Shann licked his lips and tasted the sting of sap smeared on his face during his struggle with the bushes. While the strip of meadow behind him now had been spotted with light plants, the cut below showed an almost solid line of them stringing willow-wise along the water's edge. To go down at this point was simply to spotlight his presence for any Throg on his trail. He could only continue along the upper bank, hoping to finally find an end to the growth of luminescent vegetation below.

Shann was perhaps five yards from the point where he had come to the river, when a commotion behind made him freeze and turn his head cautiously. The camp was half hidden, and the fires there must be dying. But a twisting, struggling mass was rolling across the meadow in his general direction.

Thorvald fighting off an attack? The wolverines? Shann drew his legs under him, ready to erupt into a counter-offensive. He hesitated between drawing stunner or knife. In his brush with the injured Throg at the wreck the stunner had had little impression on the enemy. And now he wondered if his blade, though it was super-steel at its toughest, could pierce any joint in the armored bodies of the aliens.

There was surely a fight in progress. The whole crazily weaving blot collapsed and rolled down upon three bright light plants. Dull sheen of Throg casing was revealed . . . no sign of fur, or flesh, or clothing. Two of the aliens battling? But why?

One of those figures got up stiffly, bent over the huddle still on the ground, and pulled at something. The wooden shaft of Shann's spear was wanly visible. And the form on the ground did not stir as that was jerked loose. The Throg leader dead? Shann hoped so. He slid his knife back into the sheath, tapped the hilt to make sure it was firmly in place, and crawled on. The river, twisting here and there, was a promising pool of dusky shadow ahead. The bank of willow things was coming to an end, and none too soon. For when he glanced back again he saw another Throg run across the meadow, and he watched them lift their fellow, carrying him back to camp.

The Throgs might seem indestructible, but he had put an end to one, aided by luck and a very rough weapon. With that to bolster his self-confidence to a higher notch, Shann dropped by cautious degrees over the bank and down to the water's edge. When his boots splashed into the oily flood he began to tramp downstream, feeling the pull of the water, first ankle high and then about his calves. This early in the season they did not have to fear floods, and hereabouts the stream was wide and shallow, save in mid-current at the center point.

Twice more he had to skirt patches of light plants, and once a young tree stood bathed in radiance with a pinkish tinge instead of the usual ghostly gray. Within the haze which tented the drooping branches, flitted small glittering, flying things; and the scent of its half-open buds was heavy on the air, neither pleasant nor unpleasant in Shann's nostrils, merely different.

He dared to whistle, a soft call he hoped would carry along the cut between the high banks. But, though he paused and listened until it seemed that every cell in his thin body was occupied in that act, he heard no answering call from the wolverines, nor any suggestion that either the animals or Thorvald were headed in the direction of the raft.

What was he going to do is none of the others joined him downstream? Thorvald had said not to linger there past daylight. Yet Shann knew that unless he actually sighted a Throg patrol splashing after him he would wait until he made sure of the others' fate. Both Taggi and Togi were as important to him as the Survey officer. Perhaps more so, he told himself now, because he understood them to a certain degree and found companionship in their undemanding company which he could not claim from the man.

Why *did* Thorvald insist upon their going on to the seashore? To Shann's mind his own first plan of holing up back in the eastern mountains was better. Those heights had as many hiding places as the fiord country. But Thorvald had suddenly become so set on this westward trek that he had given in. As much as he inwardly-rebelled when he took them, he found himself obeying the older man's orders. It was only when he was alone, as now, that he began to question both Thorvald's motives and his authority.

Three sprigs of a light bush set in a triangle. Shann paused and then climbed out on the bank, shaking the water from his boots as Taggi might shake such drops from a furred limb. This was the sign they had set to mark their rendezvous point, but . . .

Shann whirled, drawing his stunner. The raft was a dark blob on the surface of the water some feet farther on. And now it was bobbing up and down violently. That was not the result of any normal tug of current. He heard an indignant squeal and relaxed with a little laugh. He need not have worried about the wolverines; that bait had drawn them all right. Both of them were now engaged in eating, though they had to conduct their feast on the rather shaky foundation of the makeshift transport.

They paid no attention as he waded out, pulling at the anchor cord as he went. The wind must have carried his familiar scent to them. As the water climbed to his shoulders Shann put one hand on the outmost log of the raft. One of the animals snarled a warning at being disturbed. Or had that been at him?

Shann stood where he was, listening intently. Yes, there was a splashing sound from upstream. Whoever followed his own recent trail was taking no care to keep that pursuit a secret, and the pace of the newcomer was fast enough to spell trouble.

Throgs? Tensely the Terran waited for some reaction from the wolverines. He was sure that if the aliens had followed him, both animals would give warning. Save when they had gone wild upon hearing that strange wail from the camp, they avoided meeting the enemy.

But from all sounds the animals had not stopped feeding. So the other was no beetle-head. On the other hand, why would Thorvald so advertise his coming, unless the need for speed was greater than caution? Shann drew taut the mooring cord, bringing out his knife to saw through that tough length. A figure passed the three-sprig signal, ran onto the raft.

"Lantee?" The call came in a hoarse, demanding whisper.

"Here."

"Cut loose. We have to get out of here!"

Thorvald flung himself forward, and together the men scrambled up on the raft. The mangled carcass plunged into the water, dislodged by their efforts. But before the wolverines could follow it, the mooring vine snapped, and the river current took them. Feeling the raft sway

43

and begin to spin, the wolverines whined, crouched in the middle of what now seemed a very frail craft.

Behind them, far away but too clear, sounded that eerie howling, topping the sigh of the night wind.

"I saw—" Thorvald gasped, pausing as if to catch full lungfuls of air to back his words, "they have a 'hound!' That's what you hear."

5. PURSUIT

As THE raft revolved slowly it also slipped downstream at a steadily increasing pace, for the current had them in hold. The wolverines pressed close to Shann until the musky scent of their fur, their animal warmth, enveloped him. One growled deep in its throat, perhaps in answer to that wind-borne wail.

"Hound?" Shann asked.

Beside him in the dark Thorvald was working loose one of the poles they had readied to help control the raft's voyaging. The current carried them along, but there was a need for those lengths of sapling to fend them free from rocks and water-buried snags.

"What hound?" the younger man demanded more sharply when there came no immediate answer.

"The Throgs' tracker. But why did they import one?" Thorvald's puzzlement was plain in his tone. He added a moment later, with some of his usual firmness, "We may be in for bad trouble now. Use of a hound means an attempt to take prisoners—"

"Then they do not know that we are here, as Terrans, I mean?"

Thorvald seemed to be sorting out his thoughts when

e replied to that. "They could have brought a hound
ere just on chance that they might miss one of us in the
nitial mop-up. Or, if they believe we are natives, they
ould want a specimen for study."

"Wouldn't they just blast down Terrans on sight?"

Shann saw the dark blot which was Thorvald's head
hake in negation.

"They might need a live Terran—badly and soon."

"Why?"

"To operate the camp-call beam."

Shann's momentary bewilderment vanished. He knew
nough of Survey procedure to guess the reason for such
a move on the part of the aliens.

"The settler transport?"

"Yes, the ship. She won't planet here without the
oroper signal. And the Throgs can't give that. If they
don't take her, their time's run out before they have even
made a start here."

"But how could they know that the transport is nearly
due? When we intercept their calls they're pure gibberish
o us. Can they read our codes?"

"The supposition is that they can't. Only, concerning
Throgs, all we know is supposition. Anyway, they do
know the routine for establishing a Terran colony, and
we can't alter that proceudre except in small noncssen-
ials," Thorvald said grimly. "If that transport doesn't
pick up the proper signal to set down here on schedule,
her captain will call in the patrol escort . . . then exit one
Throg base. But if the beetle-heads can trick the ship in
and take her, then they'll have a clear five or six more
months here to consolidate their own position. After that
it would take more than just one patrol cruiser to clear
Warlock; it will require a fleet. So the Throgs will have
another world to play with, and an important one. This
lies on a direct line between the Odin and Kulkulkan

systems. A Throg base on such a trade route could eventually cut us right out of this quarter of the galaxy."

"So you think they want to capture us in order to bring the transport in?"

"By our type of reasoning, that would be a logical move—*if* they know we are here. They haven't too many of those hounds, and they don't risk them on petty jobs. I'd hoped we'd covered our trail well. But we had to risk that attack on the camp . . . I needed the map case!" Again Thorvald might have been talking to himself. "Time . . . and the right maps—" he brought his fist down on the raft, making the platform tremble—"that's what I have to have now."

Another patch of light-willows stretched along the riverbanks, and as they sailed through that ribbon of ghostly radiance they could see each other's faces. Thorvald's was bleak, hard, his eyes on the stream behind them as if he expected at any moment to see a Throg emerge from the surface of the water.

"Suppose that thing—" Shann pointed upstream with his chin— "follows us? What is it anyway?" Hound suggested Terran dog, but he couldn't stretch his imagination to believe in a working co-operation between Throg and any mammal.

"A rather spectacular combination of toad and lizard, with a few other grisly touches, is about as close as you can get to a general description. And that won't be too accurate, because like the Throgs its remote ancestors must have been of the insect family. If the thing follows us, and I think we can be sure that it will, we'll have to take steps. There is always this advantage—those hounds cannot be controlled from a flyer, and the beetle-heads never take kindly to foot slogging. So we won't have to expect any speedy chase. If it slips its masters in rough country, we can try to ambush it." In the dim light Thor-

ald was frowning. "I flew over the territory ahead on
wo sweeps, and it is a queer mixture. If we can reach the
ough country bordering the sea, we'll have won the first
ound. I don't believe that the Throgs will be in a hurry
o track us in there. They'll try two alternatives to chasing
s on foot. One, use their energy beams to rake any
uspect valley, and since there are hundreds of valleys all
retty much alike, that will take some time. Or they can
ttempt to shake us out with a dumdum should they have
ne here, which I doubt."

Shann tensed. The stories of the effects of the Throg's
umdum weapon were anything but pretty.

"And to get a dumdum," Thorvald continued as if he
were discussing a purely theoretical matter and not a
reat of something worse than death. "They'll have to
ring in one of their major ships. Which they will hesitate
o do with a cruiser near at hand. Our own danger spot
ow is the section we should strike soon after dawn to-
norrow if the rate of this current is what I have timed it.
here is a band of desert on this side of the mountains.
he river gorge deepens there and the land is bare. Let
hem send a ship over and we could be as visible as if we
vere sending up flares."

"How about taking cover now and going on only at
ight?" suggested Shann.

"Ordinarily, I'd say yes. But with time pressing us now,
o. If we keep straight on, we could reach the foothills in
bout forty hours, maybe less. And we have to stay with
he river. To strike across country there without good
upplies and on foot is sheer folly."

Two days. With perhaps the Throgs unleashing their
ound on land, combing from their flyers. With a
esert . . . Shann put out his hands to the wolverines.
he prospect certainly didn't seem anywhere near as
imple as it had the night before when Thorvald had

47

planned this escape. But then the Survey officer had le:
out quite a few points which were not pertinent. Was h
also leaving out other essentials? Shann wanted to as]
but somehow he could not.

After a while he dozed, his head resting on his knee:
He awoke, roused out of a vivid dream, a dream so de
tailed and so deeply impressed in a picture on his min
that he was confused when he blinked at the riverban
visible in the half-light of early dawn.

Instead of that stretch of earth and ragged vegetatio
now gliding past him as the raft angled along, he shoul
have been fronting a vast skull stark against the sky—
skull whose outlines were oddly inhuman, from whos
eyeholes issued and returned flying things while it
sharply protruding lower jaw was lapped by water. I
color that skull had been a violent clash of blood-red an
purple. Shann blinked again at the riverbank, seein
transposed on it still that ghostly haze of bone-bar
dome, cavernous eyeholes and nose slit, fanged jaw:
That skull was a mountain, or a mountain was a skull—
and it was important to him; he must locate it!

He moved stiffly, his legs and arms cramped but no
cold. The wolverines stirred on either side of him. Thor
vald continued to sleep, curled up beyond, the pole sti]
clasped in his hands. A flat map case was slung by a stra;
about his neck, its thin envelope between his arm and hi
body as if for safekeeping. On the smooth flap was th
Survey seal, and it was fastened with a finger lock.

Thorvald had lost some of the bright hard surface h
had shown at the spaceport where Shann had firs
sighted him. There were hollows in his cheeks, sendin;
into high relief those bone ridges beneath his eye sockets
giving him a faint resemblance to the skull of Shann'
dream. His face was grimed, his field uniform stainec
and torn. Only his hair was as bright as ever.

48

Shann smeared the back of his hand across his own face, not doubting that he must present an even more disreputable appearance. He leaned forward cautiously to look into the water, but that surface was not quiet enough to act as a mirror.

Getting to his feet as the raft bobbed under his shift of weight, Shann studied the territory now about them. He could not match Thorvald's inches, just as he must have a third less bulk than the officer, but standing, he could sight something of what now lay beyond the rising banks of the cut. That grass which had been so thick in the meadowlands around the camp had thinned into separate clumps, pale lavender in color. And the scrawniness of stem and blade suggested dehydration and poor soil. The earth showing between those clumps was not of the usual blue, but pallid, too, bleached to gray, while the bushes along the stream's edge were few and smaller. They must have crossed the line into the desert Thorvald had promised.

Shann edged around to face west. There was light enough in the sky to sight tall black pyramids waiting. They had to reach those distant mountains, mountains whose feet on the other side were resting in sea water. He studied them carefully, surveying each peak he could separate from its fellows.

Did the skull lie among them? The conviction that the place he had seen in his dreams was real, that it was to be found on Warlock, persisted. Not only was it a definite feature of the landscape somewhere in the wild places of this world, but it was also necessary for him to locate it. Why? Shann puzzled over that, with a growing uneasiness which was not quite fear, not yet, anyway.

Thorvald moved. The raft tilted and the wolverines became growly. Shann sat down, one hand out to the officer's shoulder in warning. Feeling that touch Thorvald

49

shifted, one hand striking out blindly in a blow which Shann was just able to avoid while with the other he pinned the map case yet tighter to him.

"Take it easy!" Shann urged.

The other's eyelids flicked. He looked up, but not as if he saw Shann at all.

"The Cavern of the Veil—" he muttered. "Utgard . . ." Then his eyes did focus and he sat up, gazing around him with a frown.

"We're in the desert," Shann announced.

Thorvald got up, balancing on feet planted a little apart, looking to the faded expanse of the waste spreading from the river cut. He stared at the mountains before he squatted down to fumble with the lock of the map case.

The wolverines were growing restless, though they still did not try to move about too freely on the raft, greeting Shann with vocal complaint. He and Thorvald could satisfy their hunger with a handful of concentrates from the survival kit. But those dry tablets could not serve the animals. Shann studied the terrain with more knowledge than he had possessed a week earlier. This was not hunting land, but there remained the bounty of the river.

"We'll have to feed Taggi and Togi," he broke the silence abruptly. "If we don't, they'll be into the river and off on their own."

Thorvald glanced up from one of the tough, thin sheets of map skin, again as if he had been drawn back from some distance. His eyes moved from Shann to the unpromising shore.

"How? With what?" he wanted to know. Then the real urgency of the situation must have penetrated his mental isolation. "You have an idea—?"

"There's those fish we found them eating back by the mountain stream," Shann said, recalling an incident of a few days earlier. "Rocks here, too, like those the fish were hiding under. Maybe we can locate some of them here."

He knew that Thorvald would be reluctant to work the raft in shore, to spare time-for such hunting. But there would be no arguing with hungry wolverines, and he did not propose to lose the animals for the officer's whim.

However, Thorvald did not protest. They poled the raft out of the main pull of the current, sending it in toward the southern shore in the lee of a clump of light-willows. Shann scrambled ashore, the wolverines after him, sniffing along at his heels while he overturned likely looking rocks to unroof some odd underwater dwellings. The fish with the rudimentary legs were present and not agile enough even in their native element to avoid well-clawed paws which scooped them neatly out of the river shallows. There was also a sleek furred creature with a broad flat head and paddle-equipped forepaws, rather like a miniature seal, which Taggi appropriated before Shann had a chance to examine it closely. In fact, the wolverines wrought havoc along a half-mile section of bank before the Terran could coax them back to the raft.

As they hunted, Shann got a better idea of the land about the river. It was sere, the vegetation dwindling except for some rough spikes of things pushing through the parched ground like flayed fingers, their puffed red-ness in contrast to the usual amethystine coloring of War-lock's growing things. Under the climbing sun that whole stretch of country was revealed in a stark bareness which at first repelled, and then began to interest him.

He discovered Thorvald standing on the upper bluff, looking out toward the waiting mountains. The officer turned as Shann urged the wolverines to the raft, and when he jumped down the drop to join them, Shann saw he carried a map strip unrolled in his hand.

"The situation is not as good as we hoped," he told the

younger man. "We'll have to leave the river to cross the heights."

"Why?"

"There's rapids—ending in a falls." The officer squatted down, spreading out the strip and making stabs at it with a nervous finger tip. "Here we have to leave. This is all rough ground. But lying to the south there's a gap which may be a pass. This was made from an aerial survey."

Shann knew enough to realize to what extent such a guide could go wrong. Main features of the landscape would be clear enough from aloft, but there might be unsurmountable difficulties at ground level which were not distinguishable from the air. Yet Thorvald had planned this journey as if he had already explored their escape route and that it was as open and easy as a stroll down Tyr's main transport way. Why was it so necessary that they try to reach the sea? However, since he had no objection to voice except a dislike for indefinite information, Shann did not question the other's calm assumption of command, not yet, anyway.

As they embarked and worked back into the current, Shann studied his companion. Thorvald had freely listed the difficulties lying before them. Yet he did not seem in the least worried about their being able to win through to the sea—or if he was, his outer shell of unconcern remained uncracked. Before their first day together had ended, the younger Terran had learned that to Thorvald he was only another tool, to be used by the Survey officer in some project which the other believed of primary importance. And his resentment of the valuation was under control so far. He valued Thorvald's knowledge, but the other's attitude chilled and rebuffed his need for something more than a half partnership of work.

Why had Thorvald come back to Warlock in the first place? And why had it been necessary for him to risk his life—perhaps more than his life if their theory was correct concerning the Throgs' wish to capture a Terran—to get that set of maps from the plundered camp? When he had first talked of that raid, his promised loot had been supplies to fill their daily needs; there had been no mention of maps. By all signs Thorvald was engaged on some mission. And what would happen if he, Shann, suddenly stopped being the other's obedient underling and demanded a few explanations here and now?

Only Shann knew enough about men to also know that he would not get any information out of Thorvald that the latter was not ready to give, and that such a showdown, coming prematurely, would only end in his own discomfiture. He smiled wryly now, remembering his emotions when he had first seen Ragnar Thorvald months ago. As if the officer ever considered the likes, dislikes—or dreams—of one Shann Lantee. No, reality and dreams seldom approached each other. Dreams . . .

"On any of those shoreline maps," he asked suddenly, "do they have marked a mountain shaped like a skull?"

Thorvald thrust with his pole. "Skull?" he repeated, a little absently, as he so often did in answer to Shann's questions unless they dealt with some currently important matter.

"A queer sort of skull," Shann said. Just as vividly as when he had first awakened, he could picture that skull mountain with the flying things about its eye sockets. And that, too, was odd; dream impressions usually faded with the passing of waking hours. "It has a protruding jaw and the waves wash that . . . red-and-purple rock—"

"What?"

He had Thorvald's complete attention now.

"Where did you hear about it?" That demand followed quickly.

"I didn't hear about it. I dreamed of it last night. I

stood there right in front of it. There were birds—or things flying like birds—going in and out of the eye-holes—"

"What else?" Thorvald leaned across his pole, his eyes alive, avid, as if he would pull the reply he wanted out of Shann by force.

"That was all I remember—the skull mountain." He did not add his other impression, that he was meant to find that skull, that he *must* find it.

"Nothing . . ." Thorvald paused, and then spoke slowly, with a visible reluctance. "Nothing else? No cavern with a green veil—a wide green veil—strung across it?"

Shann shook his head. "Just the skull mountain."

Thorvald looked as if he didn't quite believe that, but Shann's expression must have been convincing, for he laughed shortly.

"Well, there goes one nice neat theory up in smoke!" he commented. "No, your skull doesn't appear on any of our maps, and so probably my cavern does not exist either. They may both be smoke screens—"

"What—?" But Shann never finished that query.

A wind was rising in the desert to blow across the slit which held the river, carrying with it a fine shifting of sand which coasted down into the water as a gray haze, coating men, animals, and raft, and sighing as snow sighs when it falls.

Only that did not drown out another cry, a thin cry, diluted by the miles of land stretching behind them, but yet carrying that long ululating howl they had heard in the Throg camp. Thorvald grinned mirthlessly.

"The hound's on trail."

He bent to the pole, using it to aid the pace of the current. Shann chilled in spite of the sun's heat, followed his example, wondering if time had ceased to fight on their side.

6. THE HOUND

THE sun was a harsh ball of heat baking the ground and then, in some odd manner, drawing back that same fieriness. In the coolness of the eastern mountains Shann would not have believed that Warlock could hold such heat. The men discarded their jackets early as they swung to dip the poles. But they dared not strip off the rest of their clothing lest their skin burn. And again gusts of wind now drove sand over the edge of the cut to blanket the water.

Shann wiped his eyes, pausing in his eternal push-push, to look at the rocks which they were passing in threatening proximity. For the slash which held the river had narrowed. And the rock of its walls was naked of earth, save for sheltered pockets holding the drift of sand dust, while boulders of all sizes cut into the path of the flowing water.

He had not been mistaken; they were going faster, faster even than their efforts with the poles would account for. With the narrowing of the bed of the stream, the current was taking on a new swiftness. Shann said as much and Thorvald nodded.

"We're approaching the first of the rapids."

"Where we get off and walk around," Shann croaked wearily. The dust gritted between his teeth, irritated his eyes. "Do we stay beside the river?"

"As long as we can," Thorvald replied somberly. "We have no way of transporting water."

Yes, a man could live on very slim rations of food, continue to beat his way over a bad trail if he had the concentrate tablets they carried. But there was no going without water, and in this heat such an effort would finish them quickly. Always they both listened for another cry from behind, a cry to tell them just how near the Throg hunting party had come.

"No Throg flyers yet," Shann observed. He had expected one of those black plates to come cruising the moment the hound had pointed the direction for their pursuers.

"Not in a storm such as this." Thorvald, without releasing his hold on the raft pole, pointed with his chin to the swirling haze cloaking the air above the cut walls. Here the river dug yet deeper into the beginning of a canyon. They could breathe better. The dust still sifted down but not as thickly as a half hour earlier. Though over their heads the sky was now a grayish lid, shutting out the sun, bringing a portion of coolness to the travelers.

The Survey officer glanced from side to side, watching the banks as if hunting for some special mark or sign. At last he used his pole as a pointer to indicate a rough pile of boulders ahead. Some former landslide had quarter dammed the river at that point, and the drift of seasonal floods was caught in and among the rocky pile to form a prickly peninsula.

"In there—"

They brought the raft to shore, fighting the faster current. The wolverines, who had been subdued by the heat and the dust, flung themselves to the rocks with the eagerness of passengers deserting a sinking ship for certain rescue. Thorvald settled the map case more securely between his arm and side before he took the same leap.

When they were all ashore he prodded the raft out into the stream again, pushing the platform along until it was sucked by the current past the line of boulders.

"Listen!"

But Shann had already caught that distant rumble of sound. It was steady, beating like some giant drum. Certainly it did not herald a Throg ship in flight and it came from ahead, not from their back trail.

"Rapids . . . perhaps even the falls," Thorvald interpreted that faint thunder. "Now, let's see what kind of a road we can find here."

The tongue of boulders, spiked with driftwood, was firmly based against the wall of the cut. But it sloped up to within a few feet of the top of that gap, more than one landslide having contributed to its fashioning. The landing stage paralleled the river for perhaps some fifty feet. Beyond it water splashed a straight wall. They would have to climb and follow the stream along the top of the embankment, maybe being forced well away from the source of the water.

By unspoken consent they both knelt and drank deeply from their cupped hands, splashing more of the liquid over their heads, washing the dust from their skins. Then they began to climb the rough assent up which the wolverines had already vanished. The murk above them was less solid, but again the fine grit streaked their faces, embedding itself in their hair.

Shann paused to scrape a film of mud from his lips and chin. Then he made the last pull, bracing his slight body against the push of the wind he met there. A palm struck hard between his shoulders, nearly sending him sprawling. He had only wits enough left to recognize that as an order to get on, and he staggered ahead until rock arched over him and the sand drift was shut off.

His shoulder met solid stone, and having rubbed the

sand from his eyes, Shann realized he was in a pocket in the cliff walls. Well overhead he caught a glimpse of natural amber sky through a slit, but here was a twilight which thickened into complete darkness.

There was no sign of wolverines. Thorvald moved along the pocket southward, and Shann followed him. Once more they faced a dead end. For the crevice, with the sheer descent to the river on the right, the cliff wall at its back, came to an abrupt stop in a drop which caught at Shann's stomach when he ventured to look down.

If some battleship of the interstellar fleet had aimed a force beam across the mountains of Warlock, cutting down to what lay under the first envelope of planet-skin, perhaps the resulting wound might have resembled that slash. What had caused such a break between the height on which they stood and the much taller peak beyond, Shann could not guess. But it must have been a cataclysm of spectacular dimensions. There was certainly no descending to the bottom of that cut and reclimbing the rock face on the other side. The fugitives would either have to return to the river with all its ominous warnings of trouble to come, or find some other path across that gap which now provided such an effective barrier to the west.

"Down!" Just as Thorvald had pushed him out of the murk of the dust storm into the crevice, so now did that officer jerk Shann from his feet, forcing him to the floor of the half cave from which they had partially emerged.

A shadow moved across the bright band of sunlit sky.

"Back!" Thorvald caught at Shann again, his greater strength prevailing as he literally dragged the younger man into the dusk of the crevice. And he did not pause, nor allow Shann to do so, even when they were well undercover again. At last they reached the dark hole in the southern wall which they had passed earlier. And a push from Thorvald sent his companion into that.

Then a blow greater than any the Survey officer had aimed at him struck Shann. He was hurled against a rough wall with impetus enough to explode the air from his lungs, the ensuing pain so great that he feared his ribs had given under that thrust. Before his eyes fire lashed down the slit, searing him into temporary blindness. That flash was the last thing he remembered as thick darkness closed in, shutting him into the nothingness of unconsciousness.

It hurt to breathe; he was slowly aware first of that pain and then the fact that he *was* breathing, that he had to endure the pain for the sake of breath. His whole body was jarred into a dull torment as a weight pressed upon his twisted legs. Then strong animal breath puffed into his face. Shann lifted one hand by will power, touched thick fur, felt the rasp of a tongue laid wetly across his fingers.

Something close to terror engulfed him for a second or two when he knew that he could not see! The black about him was colored by jagged flashes of red which he somehow guessed were actually inside his eyes. He groped through that fire-pierced darkness. An animal whimper from the throat of the shaggy body pressed against him; he answered that movement.

"Taggi?"

The shove against him was almost enough to pin him once more to the wall, a painful crush on his aching ribs, as the wolverine responded to his name. That second nudge from the other side must be Togi's bid for attention.

But what had happened? Thorvald had hurled him back just after that shadow had swung over the ledge. That shadow! Shann's wits quickened as he tried to make sense of what he could remember. A Throg ship! Then that fiery lash which had cut after them could only have resulted from one of those energy bolts such as had wiped out the others of his kind at the camp. But he was still alive—!

"Thorvald?" He called through his personal darkness. When there was no answer, Shann called again, more urgently. Then he hunched forward on his hands and knees, pushing Taggi gently aside, running his hands over projecting rocks, uneven flooring.

His fingers touched what could only be cloth, before they met the warmth of flesh. And he half threw himself against the supine body of the Survey officer, groping awkwardly for heartbeat, for some sign that the other was still living.

"What—?" The one word came thickly, but Shann gave something close to a sob of relief as he caught the faint mutter. He squatted back on his heels, pressed his forearm against his aching eyes in a kind of fierce will to see.

Perhaps that pressure did relieve some of the blackout, for when he blinked again, the complete dark and the fiery trails had faded to gray, and he was sure he saw dimly a source of light to his left.

The Throg ship had fired upon them. But the aliens could not have used the full force of their weapon or neither of the Terrans would still be alive. Which meant, Shann's thoughts began to make sense—sense which brought apprehension—the Throgs probably intended to disable rather than kill. They wanted prisoners, just as Thorvald had warned.

How long did the Terrans have before the aliens would come to collect them? There was no fit landing place hereabouts for their flyer. The beetle-heads would have to set down at the edge of the desert land and climb the mountains on foot. And the Throgs were not good at that. So, the fugitives still had a measure of time.

Time to do what? The country itself held them securely captive. That drop to the southwest was one barrier. To retreat eastward would mean running straight into the hands of the hunters. To descend again to the river, their raft gone, was worse than useless. There was only this side pocket in which they sheltered. And once the Throgs arrived, they could scoop the Terrans out at their leisure, perhaps while stunned by a controlling energy beam.

"Taggi? Togi?" Shann was suddenly aware that he had not heard the wolverines for some time.

He was answered by a weirdly muffled call—from the south! Had the animals found a new exit? Was this niche more than just a niche? A cave of some length, or even a passage running back into the interior of the peaks? With that faint hope spurring him, Shann bent again over Thorvald, able now to make out the other's huddled form. Then he drew the torch from the inner loop of his coat and pressed the lowest stud.

His eyes smarted in answer to that light, watered until tears patterned the grime and dust on his cheeks. But he could make out what lay before them, a hole leading into the cliff face, the hole which might furnish the door to escape.

The Survey officer moved, levering himself up, his eyes screwed tightly shut.

"Lantee?"

"Here. And there's a tunnel—right behind you. The wolverines went that way . . ."

To his surprise there was a thin ghost of a smile on Thorvald's usually straight-lipped mouth. "And we'd better be away before visitors arrive?"

So he, too, must have thought his way through the sequence of past action to the same conclusion concerning the Throg movements.

61

"Can you see, Lantee?" The question was painfull
casual, but a note in it, almost a reaching for reassuranc
cut for the first time through the wall which had stoo
between them from their chance meeting by the wrecke
ship.

"Better now. I couldn't when I first came to," Shan
answered quickly.

Thorvald opened his eyes, but Shann guessed that h
was as blind as he himself had been. He caught at th
officer's nearer hand, drawing it to rest on his own belt.

"Grab hold!" Shann was giving the orders now. "By th
look of that opening we had better try crawling. I've
torch on at low—"

"Good enough." The other's fingers fumbled on th
band about Shann's slim waist until they gripped tight a
his back. He started on into the opening, drawing Thor
vald by that hold with him.

Luckily, they did not have to crawl far, for shortly pas
the entrance the fault or vein they were following be
came a passage high enough for even the tall Thorvald t
travel without stooping. And then only a little later h
released his hold on Shann, reporting he could now se
well enough to manage on his own.

The torch beam caught on a wall and awoke fro
there a glitter which hurt their eyes—a green-gold cluste
of crystals. Several feet on, there was another flash o
embedded crystals. Those might promise priceles
wealth, but neither Terran paused to examine them mor
closely or touch their surfaces. From time to time Shan
whistled. And always he was answered by the wolver
ines, their calls coming from ahead. So the men con
tinued to hope that they were not walking into a tra
from which the Throgs could extract them.

"Snap off your torch a moment!" Thorvald ordered.

Shann obeyed. The subdued light vanished. Yet ther

was still light to be seen—ahead and above.

"Front door," Thorvald observed. "How do we get up?"

The torch showed them that, a narrow ladder of ledges branching off when the passage they followed took a turn to the left and east. Afterward Shann remembered that climb with wonder that they had actually made it, though their advance had been slow, passing the torch from one to another to make sure of their footing.

Shann was top man when a last spurt of effort enabled him to draw himself out into the open, his hands raw, his nails broken and torn. He sat there, stupefied with his own weariness, to stare about.

Thorvald called impatiently, and Shann reached for the torch to hold it for the officer. Then Thorvald crawled out; he, too, looked around in dull surprise.

On either side, peaks cut high into the amber of the sky. But this bowl in which the men had found refuge was rich in growing things. Though the trees were stunted, the grass grew almost as high here as it did on the meadows of the lowlands. Quartering the pocket valley, galloped the wolverines, expressing in that wild activity their delight in this freedom.

"Good campsite."

Thorvald shook his head. "We can't stay here."

And, to underline that gloomy prophesy, there issued from that hole through which they had just come, muffled and broken, but still threatening, the howl of the Throgs' hound.

The Survey officer caught the torch from Shann's hold and knelt to flash it into the interior of the passage. As the beam slowly circled that opening, he held out his other arm, measuring the size of the aperture.

"When that thing gets on a hot scent"—he snapped off the beam—"the beetle-heads won't be able to control it.

There will be no reason for them to attempt to. Tho
hounds obey their first orders: kill or capture. And I thir
this one operates on 'capture.' So they'll loose it to ru
ahead of their party."

"And we move to knock it out?" Shann relied now o
the other's experience.

Thorvald rose. "It would need a blaster on full pow
to finish off a hound. No, we can't kill it. But we ca
make it a doorkeeper to our advantage." He trotted dow
into the valley, Shann beside him without understandir
in the least, but aware that Thorvald did have some pla
The officer bent, searched the ground, and began to pu
from under the loose surface dirt one of those nets
tough vines which they had used for cords. He thrust
double handful of this hasty harvest into Shann's ho
with a single curt order: "Twist these together and mal
as thick a rope as you can!"

Shann twisted, discovering to his pleased surprise th
under pressure the vines exuded a sticky purple sa
which not only coated his hands, but also acted as a
adhesive for the vines themselves so that his task was n
nearly as formidable as it had first seemed. With his for
ax Thorvald cut down two of the stunted trees ar
stripped them of branches, wedging the poles into th
rocks about the entrance of the hole.

They were working against time, but on Thorvald
part with practiced efficiency. Twice more that cry of th
hunter arose from the depths behind them. As the weste
ing sun, almost down now, shone into the valley hollo
Thorvald set up the frame of his trap.

"We can't knock it out, any more than we can knoc
out a Throg. But a beam from a stunner ought to slow
up long enough for this to work."

Taggi burst out of the grass, approaching the hole wit
purpose. And Togi was right at his heels. Both of the

ared into that opening, drooling a little, the same eager-
ess in their pose as they had displayed when hunting.
ann remembered how that first howl of the Throg
und had drawn both animals to the edge of the occu-
ed camp in spite of their marked distaste for its alien
asters.

"They're after it too." He told Thorvald what he had
ted on the night of their sortie.

"Maybe they can keep it occupied," the other com-
ented. "But we don't want them to actually mix with it;
at might be fatal."

A clamor broke out in the interior passage. Taggi
arled, backing away a few steps before he uttered his
vn war cry.

"Ready!" Thorvald jumped to the net slung from the
les; Shann raised his stunner.

Togi underlined her mate's challenge with a series of
arls rising in volume. There was a tearing, scrambling
und from within. Then Shann fired at the jack-in-the-
ox appearance of a monstrous head, and Thorvald re-
ased the deadfall.

The thing squalled. Ropes beat, growing taut. The
olverines backed from jaws which snapped fruitlessly.
o Shann's relief the Terran animals appeared content to
ait the now imprisoned—or collared—horror, without
nturing to make any close attack.

But he reckoned that too soon. Perhaps the stunner
ad slowed up the hound's reflexes, for those jaws stilled
ith a last shattering snap, the toad-lizard mask—a head
hich was against all nature as the Terrans knew it—was
uiet in the strangle leash of the rope, the rest of the
ody serving as a cork to fill the exit hole. Taggi had
een waiting only for such a chance. He sprang, claws
ady. And Togi went in after her mate to share the
attle.

7. UNWELCOME GUIDE

THERE was a small eruption of earth and stone as th
hound came alive, fighting to reach its tormentors. Th
resulting din was deafening. Shann, avoiding by a hand
breadth a snap of jaws with power to crush his leg int
bone powder and mangled flesh, cuffed Togi across he
nose and buried his hands in the fur about Taggi's throa
as he heaved the male wolverine back from the strug
gling monster. He shouted orders, and to his surpris
Togi did obey, leaving him free to yank Taggi away
Perhaps neither wolverine had expected the full fury c
the hound.

Though he suffered a slash across the back of on
hand, delivered by the over-excited Taggi, in the en
Shann was able to get both animals away from the hol
now corked so effectively by the slavering thing. Tho:
vald was actually laughing as he watched his younge
companion in action.

"This ought to slow up the beetles! If they haul the
little doggie back, it's apt to take out some of its rage o
them, and I'd like to see them dig around it."

Considering that the monstrous head was swingin
from side to side in a collar of what seemed to be in
movable rocks, Shann thought Thorvald right. He wei
down on his knees beside the wolverines, soothing the
with hand and voice, trying to get them to obey h
orders willingly.

"Ha!" Thorvald brought his mud-stained hands to-
ether with a clap, the sharp sound attracting the atten-
on of both animals.

Shann scrambled up, swung out his bleeding hand in
he simple motion which meant to hunt, being careful to
ignal down the valley westward. Taggi gave a last reluc-
ant growl at the hound, to be answered by one of its ear-
orturing howls, and then trotted off, Togi tagging be-
ind.

Thorvald caught Shann's slashed hand, inspecting the
leeding cut. From the aid packet at his belt he brought
ut powder and a strip of protecting plasta-flesh to
leanse and bind the wound.

"You'll do," he commented. "But we'd better get out of
ere before full dark."

The small paradise of the valley was no safe campsite.
t could not be so long as that monstrosity on the hillside
ehind them roared and howled its rage to the darkening
ky. Trailing the wolverines, the men caught up with the
nimals drinking from a small spring and thankfully
hared that water. Then they pushed on, not able to for-
et that somewhere in the peaks about must lurk the
hrog flyer ready to attack on sight.

Only darkness could not be held off by the will of men.
Here in the open there was no chance to use the torch. As
ong as they were within the valley boundaries the
hosphorescent bushes marked a path. But by the com-
ng of complete darkness they were once more out in a
egion of bare rock.

The wolverines had killed a brace of skitterers, con-
uming hide and soft bones as well as the meager flesh
vhich was not enough to satisfy their hunger. However,
o Shann's relief, they did not wander too far ahead. And
s the men stopped at last on a ledge where a fall of rock
gave them some limited shelter both animals crowded in

against the humans, adding the heat of their bodies to the slight comfort of that cramped resting place.

From time to time Shann was startled out of a troubled half sleep by the howl of the hound. Luckily that sound never seemed any louder. If the Throgs had caught up with their hunter, and certainly they must have done so by now, they either could not, or would not free it from the trap. Shann dozed again, untroubled by any dreams, to awake hearing the shrieks of clak-claks. But when he studied the sky he was able to sight none of the cliff-dwelling Warlockian bats.

"More likely they are paying attention to our friend back in the valley," Thorvald said dryly, rightly reading Shann's glance to the clouds overhead. "Ought to keep them busy."

Clak-claks were meat eaters, only they preferred their chosen prey weak and easy to attack. The imprisoned hound would certainly attract their kind. And those shrill cries now belling through the mountain heights ought to draw everyone of their species within miles.

"There it is!" Thorvald, pulling himself to his feet by a rock handhold, gazed westward, his gaunt face eager.

Shann, expecting no less than a cruising Throg ship, searched for cover on their perch. Perhaps if they flattened themselves behind the fall of stones, they might be able to escape attention. Yet Thorvald made no move into hiding. And so Shann followed the line of the other's fixed stare.

Before and below them lay a maze of heights and valleys, sharp drops, and saw-toothed rises. But on the far rim of that section of badlands shone the green of a Warlockian sea rippling on to the only dimly seen horizon. They were now within sight of their goal.

Had they had one of the exploration sky-flitters from the overrun camp, they could have walked its beach

ands within the hour. Instead, they fought their way
hrough a Devil-designed country for the next two days.
'wice they had narrow escapes from the Throg ship—or
hips—which continued to sweep across the rugged line
f the coast, and only a quick dive to cover, wasting
recious time cowering like trapped animals, saved them
rom discovery. But at least the hound did not bay again
n the tangled trail they left, and they hoped that the
rap and the clak-claks had put that monster permanently
ut of service.

On the third day they came down to one of those fiords
vhich tongued inland, fringing the coast. There had been
o lack of hunting in the narrow valleys through which
hey had threaded, so both men and wolverines were
vell fed. Though animal fur wore better than the now
attered uniforms of the men.

"Now where?" Shann asked.

Would he now learn the purpose driving Thorvald on
o this coastland? Certainly such broken country afforded
;ood hiding, but no better concealment than the moun-
ains of the interior.

The Survey officer turned slowly around on tho shingle,
tudying the heights behind them as well as the angle of
he inlet where the wavelets lapped almost at their bat-
ered boot tips. Opening his treasured map case, he
egan a patient checking of landmarks against several of
he strips he carried. "We'll have to get on down to the
rue coast."

Shann leaned against the trunk of a conical branched
nountain tree, pulling absently at the shreds of wine-
olored bark being shed in seasonal change. The chill
hey had known in the upper valleys was succeeded here
by a humid warmth. Spring was becoming a summer
;uch as this northern continent knew. Even the fresh
vind, blowing in from the outer sea, had already lost

some of the bite they had felt two days before when it salt-laden mistiness had first struck them.

"Then what do we do there?" Shann persisted.

Thorvald brought over the map, his black-rimmed nai tracing a route down one of the fiords, slanting out to indicate a lace of islands extending in a beaded line across the sea.

"We head for these."

To Shann that made no sense at all. Those islands . . why, they would offer less chance of establishing a safe base than the broken land in which they now stood. Ever the survey scouts had given those spots of sea-encircled earth the most cursory examination from the air.

"Why?" he asked bluntly. So far he had followed orders because they had for the most part made sense But he was not giving obedience to Thorvald as a matter of rank alone.

"Because there is something out there, something which may make all the difference now. Warlock isn't ar empty world."

Shann jerked free a long thong of loose bark, rolling it between his fingers. Had Thorvald cracked? He knew that the officer had disagreed with the findings of the team and had been an unconvinced minority of one who had refused to subscribe to the report that Warlock had no native intelligent life and therefore was ready and waiting for human settlement because it was technically an empty world. But to continue to cling to that belief without a single concrete proof was certainly a sign of mental imbalance.

And Thorvald was regarding him now with frowning impatience. You were supposed to humor delusions, weren't you? Only, could you surrender and humor a wild idea which might mean your death? If Thorvald wanted to go island-hopping in chance of discovering what never had existed, Shann need not accompany him. And if the officer tried to use force, well, Shann was armed with a stunner, and had, he believed, more control over the wolverines. Perhaps if he merely gave lip agreement to this project . . . Only he didn't believe, noting the light deep in those gray eyes holding on him, that anybody could talk Thorvald out of this particular obsession.

"You don't believe me, do you?" The impatience arose hotly in that demand.

"Why shouldn't I?" Shann tried to temporize. "You've had a lot of exploration experience; you should know about such things. I don't pretend to be any authority."

Thorvald refolded the map and placed it in the case. Then he pulled at the sealing of his blouse, groping in an inner secret pocket. He uncurled his fingers to display his treasure.

On his palm lay a coin-shaped medallion, bone-white but possessing an odd luster which bone would not normally show. And it was carved. Shann put out a finger, though he had a strange reluctance to touch the object. When he did he experienced a sensation close to the tingle of a mild electric shock. And once he had made that contact, he was also impelled to pick up that disk and examine it more closely.

The carved pattern was very intricate and had been done with great delicacy and skill, though the whorls, oddly shaped knobs, ribbon tracings, made no connected design he could determine. After a moment or two of study, Shann became aware that his eyes, following those twists and twirls, were "fixed," that it required a distinct effort to look away from the thing. Feeling some of that same alarm as he had known when he first heard of the wailing of the Throg hound, he let the disk fall back into Thorvald's hold, even more disturbed when he discovered that to relinquish his grasp required some exercise of will.

"What is it?"

Thorvald restored the coin to his hiding place.

"You tell me. I can say this much, there is no listing for anything even remotely akin to this in the Archives."

Shann's eyes widened. He absently rubbed the fingers which had held the bone coin—if it was a coin—back and forth across the torn front of his blouse. That tingle . . . did he still feel it? Or was his imagination at work again? But an object not listed in the exhaustive Survey Archives would mean some totally new civilization, a new stellar race.

"It is definitely a created article," the Survey officer continued. "And it was found qn the beach of one of those sea islands."

"Throg?" But Shann already knew the answer to that.

"Throg work—*this?*" Thorvald was openly scornful. "Throgs have no conception of such art. You must have seen their metal plates—those are the beetle-heads' idea of beauty. Have those the slightest resemblance to this?"

"Then who made it?"

"Either Warlock has—or once had—a native race advanced enough in a well-established form of civilization to develop such a sophisticated type of art, or there have been other visitors from space here before us and the Throgs. And the latter possibility I don't believe—"

"Why?"

"Because this was carved of bone or an allied substance. We haven't been quite able to identify it in the labs, but it is basically organic material. It was found exposed to the weather and yet it is in perfect condition, could have been carved any time within the past five years. It has been handled, yes, but not roughly. And we have come across evidences of no other star-cruising races or species save ourselves and the Throgs. No, I say this was made here on Warlock, not too long ago, and by intelligent beings of a very high grade of civilization."

"But they would have cities," protested Shann. "We've been here for months, explored all over this continent. We would have seen them or some traces of them."

"An old race, maybe," Thorvald mused, "a very old race, perhaps in decline, reduced to a remnant in numbers with good reason to retire into hiding. No, we've discovered no cities, no evidence of a native culture past or present. But this—" he touched the front of his blouse —"was found on the shore of an island. We may have been looking in the wrong place for our natives."

"The sea . . ." Shann glanced with new interest at the green water surging in wavelets along the edge of the fiord.

"Just so, the sea!"

"But scouts have been here for more than a year, one team or another. And nobody saw anything or found any traces."

"All four of our base camps were set inland, our explorations along the coast were mainly carried out by flitter, except for one party—the one which found this. And there may be excellent local reasons why any native never showed himself to us. For that matter, they may not be able to exist on land at all, any more than we could live without artificial aids in the sea."

"Now—?"

"Now we must make a real attempt to find them if they do exist anywhere near here. A friendly native race could make all the difference in the world in any struggle with the Throgs."

"Then you did have more than the dreams to back you when you argued with Fenniston!" Shann cut in.

Thorvald's eyes were on him again. "When did you hear that, Lantee?"

To his great embarrassment, Shann found himself flushing. "I heard you, the day you left for Headquarters," he admitted, and then added in his own defense, "Probably half the camp did, too."

Thorvald's gathering frown flickered away. He gave a snort of laughter. "Yes, I guess we did rather get to the bellowing point that morning. The dreams—" he came back to the subject—"Yes, the dreams were—are—important. We had their warning from the start. Lorry was the First-In Scout who charted Warlock, and he is a good man. I guess I can break secret now to tell you that his ship was equipped with a new experimental device which recorded—well, you might call it an "emanation" —a radiation so faint its source could not be traced. And it registered whenever Lorry had one of those dreams. Unfortunately, the machine was very new, very much in the untested stage, and its performance when checked later in the lab was erratic enough so the powers-that-be questioned all its readings. They produced a half dozen answers to account for that tape, and Lorry only caught the recording as long as he was on a big bay to the south.

"Then when two check flights came in later, carrying perfected machines and getting no recordings, it was all written off as a mistake in the first experiment. A planet such as Warlock is too big a find to throw away when there was no proof of occupancy. And the settlement boys rushed matters right along."

Shann recalled his own vivid dream of the skull-rock set in the lap of water—this sea? And another small point fell into place to furnish the beginning of a pattern. "I was asleep on the raft when I dreamed about that skull-mountain," he said slowly, wondering if he were making sense.

Thorvald's head came up with the alert stance of Taggi on a strong game scent.

"Yes, on the raft you dreamed of a skull-rock. And I of a cavern with a green veil. Both of us were on water—water which had an eventual connection with the sea. Could water be a conductor? I wonder. . . ." Once again his hand went into his blouse. He crossed the strip of gravel beach and dipped fingers into the water, letting the drops fall on the carved disk he now held in his other hand.

"What are you doing?" Shann could see no purpose in that.

Thorvald did not answer. He had pressed wet hand to dry now, palm to palm, the coin cupped tightly between them. He turned a quarter circle, to face the still distant open sea.

"That way." He spoke with a new odd tonelessness.

Shann stared into the other's face. All the eager alertness of only a moment earlier had been wiped away. Thorvald was no longer the man he had known, but in some frightening way a husk, holding a quite different personality. The younger Terran answered his fear with an attack from the old days of rough in-fighting in the Dumps of Tyr. He brought his right hand down hard in a sharp chop across the officer's wrists. The bone coin spun to the sand and Thorvald stumbled, staggering forward a step or two. Before he could recover balance Shann had stamped on the medallion.

Thorvald whirled, his stunner drawn with a speed for which Shann gave him high marks. But the younger man's own weapon was already out and ready. And he talked—fast.

"That thing's dangerous! What did you do—what did it do to you?"

75

His demand got through to a Thorvald who was himself again.

"What was *I* doing?" came a counter demand.

"You were acting like a mind-controlled."

Thorvald stared at him incredulously, then with a growing spark of interest.

"The minute you dripped water on that thing you changed," Shann continued.

Thorvald reholstered his stunner. "Yes," he mused, "why *did* I want to drip water on it? Something prompted me . . ." He ran his still damp hand up the angle of his jaw, across his forehead as if to relieve some pain there. "What else did I do?"

"Faced to the sea and said 'that way,'" Shann replied promptly.

"And why did you move in to stop me?"

Shann shrugged. "When I first touched that thing I felt a shock. And I've seen mind-controlled—" He could have bitten his tongue for betraying that. The world of the mind-controlled was very far from the life Thorvald and his kind knew.

"Very interesting," commented the other. "For one of so few years you seem to have seen a lot, Lantee—and apparently remembered most of it. But I would agree that you are right about this little plaything; it carries a danger with it, being far less innocent than it looks." He tore off one of the fluttering scraps of rag which now made up his sleeve. "If you'll just remove your foot, we'll put it out of business for now."

He proceeded to wrap the disk well in his bit of cloth, taking care not to touch it again with his bare fingers while he stowed it away.

"I don't know what we have in this—a key to unlock a door, a trap to catch the unwary. I can't guess how or why it works. But we can be reasonably sure it's not just some carefree maiden's locket, nor the equivalent of a credit to spend in the nearest bar. So it pointed me to the sea, did it? Well, that much I am willing to allow. Maybe we'll be able to return it to the owner, *after* we learn who—or what—that owner is."

Shann gazed down at the green water, opaque, not to be pierced to the depths by human sight. Anything might lurk there. Suddenly the Throgs became normal when balanced against an unknown living in the murky depths of an aquatic world. Another attack on the Throg-held camp could be well preferred to such exploration as Thorvald had in mind. Yet Shann did not voice any protest as the Survey officer faced again in the same direction as the disk had pointed him moments before.

8. UTGARD

A WIND from the west sprang up an hour before sunset, lashing waves inland until their spray was a salt mist in the air, a mist to sodden clothing, plaster hair to the skull, leaving a brine slime across the skin. Yet Thorvald hunted no shelter in spite of the promise in the rough shoreline at their backs. The sand in which their boots slipped and slid was coarse stuff, hardly finer than gravel, studded with nests of drift—bone-white or grayed or pale lavender—smoothed and stored by the seasons of low tides and high, seasonal storms and hurricanes. A wild shore and a forbidding one, to arouse Shann's distrust, perhaps a fitting goal for that disk's guiding.

Shann had tasted loneliness in the mountains, experienced the strange world of the river at night lighted by the wan radiance of glowing shrubs and plants, forced the starkness of the heights. Yet there had been through all that journeying a general resemblance to his own past on other worlds. A tree was a tree, whether it bore purple foliage or was red-veined. A rock was a rock, a river a river. They were equally hard and wet on Warlock or Tyr.

But now a veil he could not describe, even in his own thoughts, hung between him and the sand over which he walked, between him and the sea which sent spray to wet his torn clothing, between him and that wild wrack of long-ago storms. He could put out his hand and touch sand, drift, spray; yet they were a setting where something lay hidden behind that setting—something watched, calculatingly, with intelligence, and a set of emotions and values he did not, could not share.

". . . storm coming." Thorvald paused in the buffeting of wind and spray, watching the fury of the tossing sea. The sun was still a pale smear just above the horizon. And it gave light enough to make out that trickle of islands melting out to obscurity.

"Utgard—"

"Utgard?" Shann repeated, the strange world holding no meaning for him.

"Legend of my people." Thorvald smeared spray from his face with one hand. "Utgard, those outermost islands where dwell the giants who are the mortal enemies of the old gods."

Those dark lumps, most of them bare rock, only a few crowned with stunted vegetation, might well harbor *any-thing*, Shann decided, giants or the malignant spirits of any race. Perhaps even the Throgs had their tales of evil things in the night, beetle monsters to people wild, unknown lands. He caught at Thorvald's arm and suggested a practical course of action.

"We'll need shelter before the storm strikes." To Shann's relief the other nodded.

They trailed back across the beach, their backs now to the sea and Utgard. That harsh-sounding name did so well fit the line of islands and islets, Shann repeated it to himself. Here the beach was narrow, a strip of blue sand-gravel walled by wave-worn boulders. And from that barrier of stones piled into a breastwork by chance, interwoven with bone-bare drift, arose the first of the cliffs, Shann studied the terrain with increasing uneasiness. To be caught between a sea, whipped inland by a storm wind, and that cliff would be a risk he did not like to consider, as ignorant of field lore as he was. They must locate some break nearer than the fiord down which they had come. And they must find it soon, before the daylight was gone and the full fury of bad weather struck.

In the end the wolverines discovered an exit, just as they had found the passage through the mountain. Taggi nosed into a darker line down the face of the cliff and disappeared, Togi duplicating that feat. Shann trailed them, finding the opening a tight squeeze.

He squirmed into dimness, his outstretched hands meeting a rough stone surface sloping upward. After gaining a point about eight feet above the beach he was able to look back and down through the seaward slit. Open to the sky the crevice proved a doorway to a narrow valley, not unlike those which housed the fiords, but provided with a thick growth of vegetation well protected by the high walls.

Working as a now well-rehearsed team, the men set up a shelter of saplings and brush, the back to the slit through which wind was still able to tear a way. Walled in by stone and knowing that no Throg flyer would attempt to fly in the face of the coming storm, they dared make a fire. The warmth was a comfort to their bodies,

just as the light of the flames, men's age-old hearth com
panion, was a comfort to the fugitives' spirits. Thos
dancing spears of red, for Shann at least, burned awa
that veil of other-worldliness which had enwrapped th
beach, providing in the night an illusion of the home h
had never really known.

But the wind and the weather did not keep truce ver
long. A wailing blast around the upper peaks produced
caterwauling to equal the voices of half a dozen Throg
hounds. And in their poor shelter the Terrans not only
heard the thunderous boom of surf, but felt the vibration
of that beat pounding through the very ground on which
they lay. The sea must have long since covered the beach
over which they had come and was now trying its
strength against the rock of the cliff barrier. They could
not talk to each other over that din, although shoulder
touched shoulder.

The last flush of amber vanished from the sky with the
speed of a dropped curtain. Tonight no period of twilight
divided night from day, but their portion of Warlock was
plunged abruptly into darkness. The wolverines crowded
into their small haven, whining deep in their throats.
Shann ran his hands along their furred bodies, trying to
give them a reassurance he himself did not feel. Never
before when on stable land had he been so aware of the
unleashed terrors nature could exert, the forces against
which all mankind's controls were as nothing.

Time could no longer be measured by any set of minutes or hours. There was only darkness, the howling
winds, and the salty rain which must be in part the
breath of the sea driven in upon them. The comforting
fire vanished, chill and dankness crept up to cramp their
bodies, so that now and again they were forced to their
feet, to swing arms, stamp, drive the blood into faster
circulation.

Later came a time when the wind died, no longer driving the rain bullet-hard against and through their flimsy shelter. Then they slept in the thick unconsciousness of exhaustion.

A red-purple skull—and from its eye sockets the flying things—kept coming . . . going . . . Shann trod on an unsteady foundation which dipped under his weight as had the raft of the river voyage. He was drawing nearer to that great head, could see now how waves curled about the angle of the lower jaw, slapping inward between gaps of missing teeth—which were really broken fangs of rock—as if the skull now and then sucked reviving moisture from the water. The aperture marking the nose was closer to a snout, and the hole was dark, dark as the empty eye sockets. Yet that darkness was drawing him past any effort to escape he could summon. And then that on which he rode so perilously was carried forward by the waves, grated against the jawbone, while against his own fighting will his hands arose above his head, reaching for a hold to draw his shrinking body up the stark surface to that snout-passage.

"Lantee!" A hand jerked him back, broke that compulsion—and the dream. Shann opened his eyes with difficulty, his lashes seemed glued to his cheeks.

He might have been surveying a submerged world. Thin streamers of fog twined up from the earth as if they grew from seeds planted by the storm. But there was no wind, no sound from the peaks. Only under his stiff body Shann could still feel that vibration which was the sea battering against the cliff wall.

Thorvald was crouched beside him, his hand still urgent on the younger man's shoulder. The officer's face was drawn so finely that his features, sharp under the tanned skin, were akin to the skull Shann still half saw among the ascending pillars of fog.

"Storm's over."

Shann shivered as he sat up, hugging his arms to his chest, his tattered uniform soggy under that pressure. He felt as if he would never be warm again. When he moved sluggishly to the pit where they had kindled their handful of fire the night before he realized that the wolverines were missing.

"Taggi—?" His voice sounded rusty in his own ears, as if some of the moisture thick in the air about them had affected his vocal cords.

"Hunting." Thorvald's answer was clipped. He was gathering a handful of sticks from the back of their lean-to, where the protection of their own bodies had kept that kindling dry. Shann snapped a length between his hands, dropped it into the pit.

When they did coax a blaze into being they stripped, wringing out their clothing, propping it piece by steaming piece on sticks by the warmth of the flames. The moist air bit at their bodies and they moved briskly, striving to keep warm by exercise. Still the fog curled, undisturbed by any shaft of sun.

"Did you dream?" Thorvald asked abruptly.

"Yes." Shann did not elaborate. Disturbing as his dream had been, the feeling that it was not to be shared was also strong, as strong as some order.

"And so did I," Thorvald said bleakly. "You saw your skull-mountain?"

"I was climbing it when you awoke me," Shann returned unwillingly.

"And I was going through my green veil when Taggi took off and wakened me. You are sure your skull exists?"

"Yes."

"And so am I that the cavern of the veil is somewhere on this world. But why?" Thorvald stood up, the firelight marking plainly the lines between his tanned arms, his

82

brown face and throat, and the paleness of his lean body. "Why do we dream those particular dreams?"

Shann tested the dryness of a shirt. He had no reason to try and explain the wherefore of those dreams, only was he certain that he would sometime, somewhere, find that skull, and that when he did he would climb to the doorway of the snout, pass behind to depths where the flying things might nest—not because he wanted to make such an expedition, but because he must.

He drew his hands across his ribs, where pressure still brought an aching reminder of the crushing force of the energy whip the Throgs had wielded. There was no extra flesh on his body, yet muscles slid easily under the skin, a darker skin than Thorvald's, deepening to a warm brown where it had been weathered. His hair, unclipped now for a month, was beginning to curl about his head in tight dark rings. Since he had always been the youngest or the smallest or the weakest in the world of the Dumps, of the Service, of the Team, Shann had very little personal vanity. He did possess a different type of pride, born of his own stubborn achievement in winning out over a long roster of discouragements, failures, and adverse odds.

"Why do we dream?" he repeated Thorvald's question. "No answer, sir." He gave the traditional reply of the Service recruit. And a little to his surprise Thorvald laughed with a tinge of real amusement.

"Where do you come from, Lantee?" He asked as if he were honestly interested.

"Tyr."

"Caldon mines." The Survey officer automatically matched planet to product. "How did you come into Survey?"

Shann drew on his shirt. "Signed on as casual labor," he returned with a spark of defiance. Thorvald had joined the Service the right way as a cadet, then a Team man, finally an officer, climbing that nice even ladder with every rung ready for him when he was prepared to mount it. What did his kind know about the labor barracks where the dull-minded, the failures, the petty criminals on the run, lived hard under a secret social system of their own? It had taken every bit of physical endurance and energy, every fraction of stubborn will Shann could summon, for him to survive his first three months in those barracks—unbroken and still eager to be Survey. He could still wonder at the unbelievable chance which had rescued him from that merely because Training Center had needed another odd hand to clean cages and feed troughs for the experimental animals.

And from the center he made a Team, because when working in a smaller group his push and attention to duty had been noticed and had paid off. Three years it had taken, but he *had* made Team stature. Not that that meant anything now. Shann pulled his boots on over the legs of rough dried coveralls and glanced up, to find Thorvald watching him with a new, questioning directness the younger man could not understand.

Shann sealed his blouse and stood up, knowing the bite of hunger, dull but persistent. It was a feeling he had had so many times in the past that now he hardly gave it a second thought.

"Supplies?" He brought the subject back to the present and the practical. What did it matter why or how one Shann Lantee had come to Warlock in the first place?

"What we have left of the concentrates we had better keep for emergencies." Thorvald made no move to open the very shrunken bag he had brought from the scoutship.

He walked over to a rocky outcrop and tugged loose a yellowish tuft of plant, neither moss nor fungi but sharing attributes of both. Shann recognized it without enthusiasm as one of the varieties of native produce which could be safely digested by Terran stomachs. The stuff was almost tasteless and possessed a rather unpleasant odor. Consumed in bulk it would satisfy hunger for a time. Shann hoped that with the wolverines to aid they could go back to hunting soon.

However, Thorvald showed no desire to head inland where they might expect to locate game. He disagreed with Shann's suggestion for tracking Taggi and Togi when those two emerged from the underbrush obviously well fed and contented after their early morning activity.

When Shann protested with some heat, the other countered: "Didn't you ever hear of fish, Lantee? After a storm such as last night's, we ought to discover good pickings along the shore."

But Shann was also sure that it was not only the thought of food which drew Thorvald back to the sea.

They crawled back through the bolt hole. The beach of gravel-sand had vanished save for a narrow ribbon of land just at the foot of the cliffs, where the water curled in white lace about the barrier of boulders. There was no change in the dullness of the sky; no sun broke through the thick lid of clouds. And the green of the sea was ashened to gray which matched that overcast until one could strain one's eyes trying to find the horizon, unable to mark the dividing line here between air and water.

Utgard was a broken necklace, the outermost island-beads lost, the inner ones more isolated by the rise in water, more forbidding. Shann let out a startled hiss of breath.

The top of a near-by rock detached itself, drew up into a hunched thing of armor-plated scales and heavy wide-jawed head. A tail cracked into the air; a double tail split into equal forks for half-way down its length. A leg lifted as a forefoot, webbed, clawed for a new hold. This sea beast was the most formidable native thing he had sighted on Warlock, approaching in its ugliness the hound of the Throgs.

Breathing in labored gusts, the thing slapped its tail down on the stones with a limpness which suggested that the raising of that appendage had overtaxed its limited supply of strength. The head sank forward, resting across one of the forelimbs. Then Shann sighted the fearsome wound in the side just before one of the larger hind legs, a ragged hole through which pumped with every one of those breaths a dark purplish stream, licked away by the waves as it trickled slickly down the rock.

"What is that?"

Thorvald shook his head. "Not on our records," he replied absently, studying the dying creature with avid attention. "Must have been driven in by the storm. This proves there is more in the sea than we knew!"

Again the forked tail lifted and fell, the head raised from the forelimb, stretching up and back until the white underfolds of the throat were exposed as the snout pointed almost vertically to the sky. The jaws opened and from between them came a moaning whistle, a complaint which was drowned out by the wash of the waves. Then, as if that was the last effort, the webbed, clawed feet relaxed their grip of the rock and the scaled body slid sidewise, out of their sight, into the water. There was a feather of spume to mark the plunge and nothing else.

Shann, watching to see if the reptile would surface again, sighted another object, a rounded shape floating on the sea, bobbing lightly as had their river raft.

"Look!"

Thorvald's gaze followed his pointing finger and then before Shann could protest, the officer leaped outward from their perch on the cliff to the broad rock where the scaled sea dweller had lain moments earlier. He stood there, watching that drifting object with the closest attention, as Shann made the same crossing in his wake.

The drifting thing was oval, perhaps some six feet long and three wide, the mid point rising in a curve from the water's edge. As far as Shann could make out in the half-light the color was a reddish-brown, the surface rough. And he thought by the way that it moved that it must be flotsam of the storm, buoyant enough to ride the waves with close to cork resiliency. To Shann's dismay his companion began to strip.

"What are you going to do?"

"Get that."

Shann surveyed the water about the rock. The forked tail had sunk just there. Was the Survey officer mad enough to think he could swim unmenaced through a sea which might be infested with more such creatures? It seemed that he was, for Thorvald's white body arched out in a dive. Shann waited, half crouched and tense, as though he could in some way attack anything rising from the depths to strike at his companion.

A brown arm flashed above the surface. Thorvald swam strongly toward the floating object. He reached it, his outstretched hand rasping across the surface. And it responded so quickly to that touch that Shann guessed it was even lighter and easier to handle than he had first thought.

Thorvald headed back, herding the thing before him. And when he climbed out on the rock, Shann was pulling up his trophy. They flipped the find over, to discover it hollow. They had, in effect, a ready-made craft not unlike a canoe with blunted bows. But the substance was surely organic. Was it shell? Shann speculated, running his finger tips over the irregular surface.

The Survey officer dressed. "We have our boat," he commented. "Now for Utgard—"

Use this frail thing to dare the trip to the islands? But Shann did not protest. If the officer determined to try such a voyage, he would do it. And neither did the younger man doubt that he would accompany Thorvald.

9. ONE ALONE

ONCE again the beach was a wide expanse of shingle, drying fast under a sun hotter than any Shann had yet known on Warlock. Summer had taken a big leap forward. The Terrans worked in partial shade below a cliff overhang, not only for the protection against the sun's rays, but also as a precaution against any roving Throg air patrol.

Under Thorvald's direction the curious shell dragged from the sea—if it were a shell, and the texture as well as the general shape suggested that—was equipped with a framework to act as a stabilizing outrigger. What resulted was certainly an odd-looking craft, but one which obeyed the paddles and rode the waves easily.

In the full sunlight the outline of islands was clearcut—red-and-gray-rock above an aquamarine sea. The Terrans had sighted no more of the sea monsters, and the major evidence of native life along the shore was a new species of clak-claks, roosting in cliff holes and scavenging along the sands, and various queer fish and shelled things stranded in small tide pools—to the delight of the wolverines, who fished eagerly up and down the beach, ready to investigate all debris of the storm.

"That should serve." Thorvald tightened the last lashing, straightening up, his fists resting on his hips, to regard the craft with a measure of pride.

Shann was not quite so content. He had matched the Survey officer in industry, but the need for haste still eluded him. So the ship—such as it was—was ready. Now they would be off to explore Thorvald's Utgard. But a small and nagging doubt inside the younger man restrained his enthusiasm over such a voyage. Fork-tail had come out of the section of ocean which they must navigate in this very crude transport. And Shann had no desire to meet an uninjured and alert fork-tail in the latter's own territory.

"Which island do we head for?" Shann kept private his personal doubts of their success. The outmost tip of that chain was only a distant smudge lying low on the water.

"The largest . . . that one with trees."

Shann whistled. Since the night of the storm the wolverines were again more amenable to the very light discipline he tried to keep. Perhaps the fury of that elemental burst had tightened the bond between men and animals, both alien to this world. Now Taggi and his mate padded toward him in answer to his summons. But would the wolverines trust the boat? Shann dared not risk their swimming, nor would he agree to leaving them behind.

Thorvald had already stored their few provisions on board. And now Shann steadied the craft against a rock which served them as a wharf, while he coaxed Taggi gently. Though the wolverine protested, he at last scrambled in, to hunch at the bottom of the shell, the picture of apprehension. Togi took longer to make up her mind. And at length Shann picked her up bodily, soothing her with quiet speech and stroking hands, to put her beside her mate.

The shell settled under the weight of the passengers, but Thorvald's foresight concerning the use of the outrigger proved right, for the craft was seaworthy. It answered readily to the dip of their paddles as they headed in a curve, keeping the first of the islands between them and the open sea for a breakwater.

From the air, Thorvald's course would have been a crooked one, for he wove back and forth between the scattered islands of the chain, using their lee calm for the protection of the canoe. About two thirds of the group were barren rock, inhabited only by clak-claks and creatures closer to true Terran birds in that they wore a body plumage which resembled feathers, though their heads were naked and leathery. And, Shann noted, the clak-claks and the birds did not roost on the same islands, each choosing their own particular home while the other species did not invade that territory.

The first large-sized island they approached was crowned by trees, but it had no beach, no approach from sea level. Perhaps it might be possible to climb to the top of the cliff walls. But Thorvald did not suggest that they try it, heading on toward the next large outcrop of land and rock.

Here white lace patterned in a ring well out from the shore to mark a circle of reefs. They nosed their way patiently around the outer circumference of that threatening barrier, hunting the entrance to the lagoon. Within, there were at least two beaches with climbable ascents to the upper reaches inland. Though Shann noted that the vegetation showing was certainly not luxuriant, the few trees within their range of vision being pallid growths, rather like those they had sighted on the fringe of the desert. Leather-headed flyers wheeled out over their canoe, coasting on outspread wings to peer down at the

Terran invaders in a manner which suggested intelligent curiosity.

A full flock gathered to escort them as they continued along the outer line of the reef. Thorvald impatiently dug his paddle deeper. They had explored more than half of the reef now without chancing on an entrance channel.

"Regular fence," Shann commented. One could begin to believe that the barrier had been deliberately reared to frustrate visitors. Hot sunshine, reflected back from the surface of the waves, burned their exposed skin, so they dared not discard their ragged clothing. And the wolverines were growing increasingly restless. Shann did not know how much longer the animals would consent to their position as passengers without raising active protest.

"How about trying the next one?" he asked, knowing at the same time his companion was not in any mood to accept such a suggestion with good will.

The officer made no reply, but continued to use his steer paddle in a fashion which spelled out his stubborn determination to find a passage. This was a personal thing now, between Ragnar Thorvald of the Terran Survey and a wall of rock, and the man's will was as strongly rooted as those water-washed stones.

On the southwestern tip of the reef they discovered a possible opening. Shann eyed the narrow space between two fanglike rocks dubiously. To him that width of water lane seemed dangerously limited, the sudden slam of a wave could dash them against either of those pillars, with disastrous results, before they could move to save themselves. But Thorvald pointed their blunt bow toward the passage with seeming confidence, and Shann knew that as far as the officer was concerned, this was their door to the lagoon.

Thorvald might be stubborn, but he was not a fool. And his training and skill in such maneuvers was proved when the canoe rode in a rising swell in and by those rocks to gain the safety, in seconds, of the calm lagoon. Shann sighed with relief, but ventured no comment.

Now they must paddle back along the inner side of the reef to locate the beaches, for fronting them on this side of the well-protected island were cliffs as formidable as those which guarded the first of the chain at which they had aimed.

Shann glanced now and then over the side of the boat, hoping in these shallows to sight the sea bed or some of the inhabitants of these waters. But there was no piercing that green murk. Here and there nodules of rock projected inches or feet above the surface, awash in the wavelets, to be avoided by the voyagers. Shann's shoulders ached and burned, his muscles were unaccustomed to the steady swing of the paddles, and the fire of the sun stabbed easily through only two layers of ragged cloth to his skin. He ran a dry tongue over dryer lips and gazed eagerly ahead in search of the first of the beaches.

What was so important about this island that Thorvald *had* to make a landing here? The officer's stories of a native race which they might turn against the Throgs to their own advantage was thin, very thin indeed. Especially now, as Shann weighed an unsupported theory against that ache in his shoulders, the possibility of being marooned on the inhospitable shore ahead, against the fifty probable dangers he could total up with very little expenditure of effort. A small nagging doubt of Thorvald's obsession began to grow in his mind. How could Shann even be sure that that carved disk and Thorvald's hokus-pokus with it had been on the level? On the other hand what motive would the officer have for trying such an act just to impress Shann?

The beach at last! As they headed the canoe in that direction the wolverines nearly brought disaster on them.

The animals' restlessness became acute as they sighted and scented the shore and knew that they were close. Taggi reared, plunged over the side of the craft, and Shann had just time to fling his weight in the opposite direction as a counterbalance when Togi followed. They splashed shoreward while Thorvald swore fluently and Shann grabbed to save the precious supply bag. In a shower of gravel the animals made land and humped well up on the strand before pausing to shake themselves and splatter far and wide the burden of moisture transported by their shaggy fur.

Ashore, the canoe became a clumsy burden and, light as the craft was, both of the men sweated to get it up on the beach without snagging the outrigger against stones and brush. With the thought of a Throg patrol in mind they worked swiftly to cover it.

Taggi raised an egg-patterned snout from a hollow and licked at the stippling of greenish yolk matting his fur. The wolverines had wasted no time in sampling the contents of a wealth of nesting places beginning just above the high-water mark, cupping two to four tough-shelled eggs in each. Treading a path among those clutches, the Terrans climbed a red-earthed slope toward the interior of the island.

They found water, not the clear running of a mountain spring, but a stalish pool in a stone-walled depression on the crest of a rise, filled by the bounty of the rain. The warm liquid was brackish, but satisfied in part their thirst, and they drank eagerly.

The outer cliff wall of the island was just that, a wall, for there was an inner slope to match the outer. And at the bottom of it a showing of purple-green foliage where plants and stunted trees fought for living space. But there was nothing else, though they quartered that growing section with the care of men trying to locate an enemy outpost.

That night they camped in the hollow, roasted eggs in a fire, and ate the fishy-tasting contents because it was food, not because they relished what they swallowed. Tonight no cloud bank hung overhead. A man, gazing up, could see the stars. The stars and other things, for over the distant shore of the mainland they sighted the cruising lights of a Throg ship and waited tensely for that circle of small sparkling points to swing out toward their own hiding hole.

"They haven't given up," Shann stated what was obvious to them both.

"The settler transport," Thorvald reminded him. "If they do not take a prisoner to talk her in and allay suspicion, then—" he snapped his fingers—"the Patrol will be on their tails, but quick!"

So just by keeping out of Throg range, they were, in a way, still fighting. Shann settled back, his tender shoulders resting against a tree bole. He tried to count the number of days and nights lying behind him now since that early morning when he had watched the Terran camp die under the aliens' weapons. But one day faded into another so that he could remember only action parts clearly—the attack on the grounded scoutship, the sortie they had made in turn on the occupied camp, the dust storm on the river, the escape from the Throg ship in the mountain crevice, and their meeting with the hound. Then that storm which had driven them to seek cover after their curious experience with the disk. And now this day when they had safely reached the island.

"Why this island?" he asked suddenly.

"That carved piece was found here on the edge of this valley," Thorvald returned matter-of-factly.

"But today we found nothing at all—"

"Yet this island supplies us with a starting point."

A starting point for what? A detailed search of all the islands, great and small, in the chain? And how did they dare continue to paddle openly from one to the next with the Throgs sweeping the skies? They would have provided an excellent target today as they combed that reef for an hour or more. Wearily, Shann spread out his hands in the very faint light of their tiny fire, poked with a finger tip at smarting points which would have been blisters had those hands not known a toughening process in the past. More paddling tomorrow? But that was tomorrow, and at least they need not worry tonight about any Throg attack once they had doused the fire, an action which was now being methodically attended to by Thorvald. Shann pushed down on the bed of leaves he had heaped together. The night was quiet. He could hear only the murmur of the sea, a lulling croon of sound to make one sleep deep, perhaps dreamlessly.

Sun struck down, making a dazzle about him. Shann turned over drowsily in that welcome heat, stretching a little as might a cat at ease. Then he really awoke under the press of memory, and the need for alertness rode him once more. Beaten-down grass, the burnt-out embers of last night's fire were beside him. But of Thorvald and the wolverines there were no signs.

Not only did he now lie alone, but he was possessed by the feeling that he had not been deserted only momentarily, that Taggi, Togi and the Survey officer were indeed gone. Shann sat up, got to his feet, breathing faster, a prickle of uneasiness spreading in him, bringing him to that inner slope, up it to the crest from which he could see that beach where last night they had concealed the canoe.

Those lengths of brush and tufts of grass they had used

for a screen were strewn about as if tossed in haste. A
not too long before . . .

For the canoe was out in the calm waters within t
reef, the paddle blade wielded by its occupant flashi
brightly in the sun. On the shingle below, the wolverin
prowled back and forth, whining in bewilderment.

"Thorvald—!"

Shann put the full force of his lungs into that ha
hearing the name ring from one of the small peaks at I
back. But the man in the boat did not turn his hea
there was no change in the speed of that paddle dip.

Shann leaped down the outer slope to the beach, ski
ding the last few feet, saving himself from going headfi
into the water only by a painful wrench of his body.

"Thorvald!" He tried calling again. But that hea
bright under the sun did not turn; there was no answe
Shann tore at his clothes and kicked off his boots.

He did not think of the possibility of lurking sea mo
sters as he plunged into the water, swam for the cano
edgeing along the reef, plainly bound for the sea gate
the southwest. Shann was not a powerful swimmer. H
first impetus gave him a good start, but after that he ha
to fight for each foot he gained, and the fear grew in hi
that the other would reach the reef passage before h
could catch up. He wasted no more time trying to ha
Thorvald, putting all his breath and energy into the effo
of overtaking the craft.

And he almost made it, his hand actually slippin
along the log which furnished the balancing outrigger. A
his fingers tightened on the slimy wood he looked up, an
loosed that hold again in time perhaps to save his life.

For when he ducked to let the water cover his head i
an impromptu half dive, Shann carried with him a vivi
picture, a picture so astounding that he was a littl
dazed.

Thorvald had stopped paddling at last, because that paddle had to be put to another use. Had Shann not released his hold on the log and gone under water, that crudely fashioned piece of wood might have broken his skull. He saw only too clearly the paddle raised in both hands as an ugly weapon, and Thorvald's face, convulsed in a spasm of rage which made it as inhuman as a Throg's.

Sputtering and choking, Shann fought up to the air once more. The paddle was back at the task for which it had been carved, the canoe was underway again, its occupant paying no more attention to what lay behind than if he *had* successfully disposed of the man in the water. To follow would be only to invite another attack, and Shann might not be so lucky next time. He was not good enough a swimmer to try any tricks such as oversetting the canoe, not when Thorvald was an expert who could easily finish off a fumbling opponent.

Shann swam wearily to shore where the wolverines waited, unable yet to make sense of that attack in the lagoon. What had happened to Thorvald? What motive had led the other to leave Shann and the animals on this island, the island Thorvald had called a starting point in his search for the natives of Warlock? Or had every bit of that tall tale been invented by the Survey officer for some obscure purpose of his own, certainly no sane purpose? Against that logic Shann could only set the carved disk, and he had only Thorvald's word that that had been discovered here.

He dragged himself out of the water on his hands and knees and lay, winded and gasping. Taggi came to lick his face, nuzzle him, making a small, bewildered whimpering. While above, the leather-headed birds called and swooped, fearful and angry for their disturbed nesting place. The Terran retched, coughed up water, and then sat up to look around.

The spread of lagoon was bare. Thorvald must have rounded the south point of land and be very close to the reef passage, perhaps through it by now. Not stopping for his clothes, Shann started up the slope, crawling part of the way on his hands and knees.

He reached the crest again and got to his feet. The sun made an eye-dazzling glitter of the waves. But under the shade of his hands Shann saw the canoe again, beyond the reef, heading on out along the island chain, not back to shore as he had expected. Thorvald was still on the hunt, but for what? A reality which existed, or a dream in his own disturbed brain?

Shann sat down. He was very hungry, for that adventure in the lagoon had sapped his strength. And he was a prisoner along with the wolverines, a prisoner on an island which was half the size of the valley which held the Survey camp. As far as he knew, his only supply of drinkable water was that tank of evil-smelling rain which would be speedily evaporated by a sun such as the one now beating down on him. And between him and the shore was the sea, a sea which harbored such creatures as the fork-tail he had watched die.

Thorvald was still steadily on course, not to the next island in the chain, a small, bare knob, but to the one beyond that. He could have been hurrying to a meeting. Where and with what?

Shann got to his feet, started down to the beach once more, sure now that the officer had no intention of returning, that he was again on his own with only his wits and strength to keep him alive—alive and somehow free of this waterwashed prison.

10. A TRAP FOR A TRAPPER

SHANN took up the piece of soft chalklike stone he had found and drew another short white mark on the rust-red of a boulder well above tide level. That made three such marks, three days since Thorvald had marooned him. And he was no nearer the shore now than he had been on that first morning! He sat where he was by the boulder, aware that he should be up, trying to climb to the less accessible nests of the sea birds. The prisoners, man and wolverines, had cleaned out all those they had discovered on beach and cliffs. But at the thought of more eggs, Shann's stomach knotted in pain and he began to retch.

There had been no sign of Thorvald since Shann had watched him steer between the two westward islands. And the younger Terran's faint hope that the officer would return had died. On the shore a few feet away lay his own pitiful attempt to solve the problem of escape.

The force ax had vanished with Thorvald, along with all the rest of the meager supplies which had been the officer's original contribution to their joint equipment. Shann had used his knife on brush and small trees, trying to put together some kind of a raft. But he had not been able to discover here any of those vines necessary for binding, and his best efforts had all come to grief when he tried them in a lagoon launching. So far he had achieved no form of raft which would keep him afloat longer than five minutes, let alone support three of them as far as the next island.

Shann pulled listlessly at the framework of his latest try, fully disheartened. He tried not to think of the unescapable fact that the water in the rain tank had sunk to only an inch or so of muddy scum. Last night he had dug in the heart of the interior valley where the rankness of the vegetation was a promise of moisture, to uncover damp clay and then a brackish ooze. Far too little to satisfy both him and the animals.

There were surely fish somewhere in the lagoon. Shann wondered if the raw flesh of sea dwellers could supply the water they needed. But lacking net, line, or hooks, how did one fish? Yesterday, using his stunner, he had brought down a bird, to discover the carcass so rank even the wolverines, never dainty eaters, refused to gnaw it.

The animals prowled the two beaches, and Shann guessed they hunted shell dwellers, for at times they dug energetically in the gravel. Togi was busied in this way now, the sand flowing from under her pumping legs, her claws raking in good earnest.

And it was Togi's excavation which brought Shann a first ray of hope. Her excitement was so marked that he believed she was in quest of some worthwhile game and he moved across to inspect the pit. A patch of brown, which had been skimmed bare by one raking paw, made him shout.

Taggi shambled downslope, going to work beside his mate with an eagerness as open as hers. Shann hovered at the edge of the pit they were rapidly enlarging. The brown patch was larger, disclosing itself as a hump doming up from the gravel. The Terran did not need to run his hands over that rough surface to recognize the nature of the find. This was another shell such as had come floating in after the storm to form the raw material of their canoe.

However, as fast as the wolverines dug, they did not appear to make correspondingly swift headway in uncovering their find as might reasonably be expected. In fact, a witness could guess that the shell was sinking at a pace only a fraction slower than the burrowers were using to free it. Intrigued by that, Shann went back to the waterline, secured one of the lengths he had been trying to weave into his failures, and returned to use it as a make-shift shovel.

Now, with three of them at the digging, the brown hump was uncovered, and Shann pried down around its edge, trying to lever it up and over. To his amazement, his tool was caught and held, nearly jerked from his hands. To his retaliating tug the obstruction below-ground gave way, and the Terran sprawled back, the length of wood coming clear, to show the other end smashed and splintered as if it had been caught between mashing gears.

For the first time he understood that they were dealing not with an empty shell casing buried by drift under this small beach, but with a shell still inhabited by the War-lockian to whom it was a natural covering, and that that inhabitant would fight to continue ownership. A moment's examination of that splintered wood also suggested that the shell's present wearer appeared well able to defend itself.

Shann attempted to call off the wolverines, but they were out of control now, digging frantically to get at this new prey. And he knew that if he pulled them away by force, they were apt to turn those punishing claws and snapping jaws on him.

It was for their protection that he returned to digging, though he no longer tried to pry up the shell. Taggi leaped to the top of that dome, sweeping paws downward to clear its surface, while Togi prowled around its circumference, pausing now and then to send dirt and gravel spattering, but treading warily as might one alert for a sudden attack.

They had the creature almost clear now, though the shell still rested firmly on the ground, and they had no notion of what it might protect. It was smaller, perhaps two thirds the size of the one which Thorvald had fashioned into a seagoing craft. But it could provide them with transportation to the mainland if Shann was able to repeat the feat of turning it into an outrigger canoe.

Taggi joined his mate on the ground and both wolverines padded about the dome, obviously baffled. Now and then they assaulted the shell with a testing paw. Claws raked and did not leave any marks but shallow scratches. They could continue that forever, as far as Shann could see, without solving the problem in the least.

He sat back on his heels and studied the scene in detail. The excavation holding the shelled creature was some three yards above the high-water mark, with a few more feet separating that from the point where lazy waves now washed the finer sand. Shann watched the slow inward slip of those waves with growing interest. Where their combined efforts had failed to win this odd battle, perhaps the sea itself could now be pressed into service.

Shann began his own excavation, a trough to lead from the waterline to the pit occupied by the obstinate shell. Of course the thing living in or under that covering might be only too familiar with salt water. But it had placed its burrow, or hiding place, above the reach of the waves and so might be disconcerted by the sudden appearance of water in its bed. However, the scheme was worth trying, and he went to work doggedly, wishing he could make the wolverines understand so they would help him.

They still prowled about their captive, scrapping at the sand about the shell casing. At least their efforts would keep the half-prisoner occupied and prevent its escape. Shann put another piece of his raft to work as a shovel, throwing up a shower of sand and gravel while sweat dampened his tattered blouse and was salt and sticky on his arms and face.

He finished his trench, one which ran at an angle he hoped would feed water into the pit rapidly once he knocked away the last barrier against the waves. And, splashing out into the green water, he did just that.

His calculations proved correct. Waves lapped, then flowed in a rapidly thickening stream, puddling out about the shell as the wolverines drew back, snarling. Shann lashed his knife fast to a stout length of sapling, so equipping himself with a spear. He stood with it ready in his hand, not knowing just what to expect. And when the answer to his water attack came, the move was so sudden that in spite of his preparation he was caught gaping.

For the shell fairly erupted out of the mess of sand and water. A complete fringe of jointed, clawed brown limbs churned in a forward-and-upward dash. But the water worked to frustrate that charge. For one of the pit walls crumbled, over-balancing the creature so that the fore end of the shell lifted from the ground, the legs clawing wildly at the air.

Shann thrust with the spear, feeling the knife point go home so deeply that he could not pull his improvised weapon free. A limb snapped claws only inches away from his leg as he pushed down on the haft with all his strength. That attack along with the initial upset of balance did the job. The shell flopped over, its rounded hump now embedded in the watery sand of the pit while the frantic struggles of the creature to right itself only buried it the deeper.

The Terran stared down upon a segmented under belly where legs were paired in riblike formation. Shann could locate no head, no good target. But he drew his stunner and beamed at either end of the oval, and then, for good measure, in the middle, hoping in one of those three general blasts to contact the thing's central nervous system. He was not to know, which of those shots did the trick, but the frantic wiggling of the legs slowed and finally ended, as a clockwork toy might run down for want of winding—and at last projected, at crooked angles, completely still. The shell creature might not be dead, but it was tamed for now.

Taggi had only been waiting for a good chance to do battle. He grabbed one of those legs, worried it, and then leaped to tear at the under body. Unlike the outer shell, this portion of the creature had no proper armor and the wolverine plunged joyfully into the business of the kill, his mate following suit.

The process of butchery was a bloody, even beastly job, and Shann was shaken before it was complete. But he kept at his labors, determined to have that shell, his one chance of escape from the island. The wolverines feasted on the greenish-white flesh, but he could not bring himself to sample it, climbing to the heights in search of eggs, and making a happy find of a niche filled with the edible moss-fungi.

By late afternoon he had the shell scooped fairly clean and the wolverines had carried away for burial such portions as they had not been able to consume at their first eating. Meanwhile, the leather-headed birds had grown bold enough to snatch up the fragments he tossed out on the water, struggling for that bounty against feeders arising from the depths of the lagoon.

At the coming of dusk Shann hauled the bloodstained, grisly trophy well up the beach and wedged it among the rocks, determined not to lose his treasure. Then he stripped and washed, first his clothing and then himself, rubbing his hands and arms with sand until his skin was tender. He was still exultant at his luck. The drift would supply him with materials for an outrigger. One more day's work—or maybe two—and he could leave. He wrung out his blouse and gazed toward the distant line of the shore. Once he had his new canoe ready he would try to make the trip back in the early morning while the mists were still on the sea. That should give him cover against any Throg flight.

That night Shann slept in the deep fog of bodily exhaustion. There were no dreams, nothing but an unconsciousness which even a Throg attack could not have pierced. He roused in the morning with an odd feeling of guilt. The water hole he had scooped in the valley yielded him some swallows tasting of earth, but he had almost forgotten the flavor of a purer liquid. Munching on a fistful of moss, he hurried down to the shore, half fearing to find the shell gone, his luck out once again.

Not only was the shell where he had wedged it, but he had done better than he knew when he had left it exposed in the night. Small things scuttled away from it into hiding, and several birds arose—scavengers had been busy lightening his unwelcome task for that morning. And seeing how the clean-up process had gone, Shann had a second inspiration.

Pushing the thing down the beach, he sank it in the shallows with several rocks to anchor it. Within a few seconds the shell was invaded by a whole school of spiny-tailed fish, that ate greedily. Leaving his find to their cleansing, Shann went back to prospect the pile of raft material, choosing pieces which could serve for an outrigger frame. He was handicapped as he had been all along by the absence of the vines one could use for lashings. And he had reached the point of considering a drastic sacrifice of his clothing to get the necessary strips when he saw Taggi dragging behind him one of the jointed legs the wolverines had put in storage the day before.

Now and again Taggi laid his prize on the shingle, holding it firmly pinned with his forepaws as he tried to worry loose a section of flesh. But apparently that feat was beyond even his notable teeth, and at length he left it lying there in disgust while he returned to a cache for more palatable fare. Shann went to examine more closely the triple-jointed limb.

The casing was not as hard as horn or shell, he discovered upon testing; it more resembled tough skin laid over bone. With a knife he tried to loosen the skin—a tedious job requiring a great deal of patience, since the tissue tore if pulled away too fast. But with care he acquired a few thongs perhaps a foot long. Using two of these, he made a trial binding of one stick to another, and experimented farther, soaking the whole construction in sea water and then exposing it to the direct rays of the sun.

When he examined his test piece an hour later, the skin thongs had set into place with such success that the one piece of wood might have been firmly glued to the other. Shann shuffled his feet in a little dance of triumph as he went on to the lagoon to inspect the water-logged shell. The scavengers had done well. One scraping, two at the most, would have the whole thing clean and ready to use.

But that night Shann dreamed. No climbing of a skull-shaped mountain this time. Instead, he was again on the beach, laboring under an overwhelming compulsion, building something for an alien purpose he could not understand. And he worked as hopelessly as a beaten slave, knowing that what he made was to his own undoing. Yet he could not halt the making, because just beyond the limit of his vision there stood a dominant will which held him in bondage.

And he awoke on the beach in the very early dawn, not knowing how he had come there. His body was bathed in sweat, as it had been during his day's labors under the sun, and his muscles ached with fatigue.

But when he saw what lay at his feet he cringed. The framework of the outrigger, close to completion the night before, was dismantled—smashed. All those strips of hide he had so laboriously culled were cut—into inch-long bits which could be of no service.

Shann whirled, ran to the shell he had the night before pulled from the water and stowed in safety. Its rounded dome was dulled where it had been battered, but there was no break in the surface. He ran his hands anxiously over the curve to make sure. Then, very slowly, he came back to the mess of broken wood and snipped hide. And he was sure, only too sure, of one thing. He, himself, had wrought that destruction. In his dream he had built to satisfy the whim of an enemy; in reality he had destroyed; and that was also, he believed, to satisfy an enemy.

The dream was a part of it. But who or what could set a man dreaming and so take over his body, make him in fact betray himself? But then, what had made Thorvald maroon him here? For the first time, Shann guessed a new, if wild, explanation for the officer's desertion. Dreams—and the disk which had worked so strangely on Thorvald. Suppose everything the other had surmised was the truth! Then that disk *had* been found on this very island, and here somewhere must lie a clue to the riddle.

Shann licked his lips. Suppose that Thorvald had been sent away under just such a strong compulsion as the one which had ruled Shann last night? Why was he left behind if the other had been moved away to protect some secret? Was it that Shann himself was wanted here, wanted so much that when he at last found a means of escape he was set to destroy it? That act might have been forced upon him for two reasons: to keep him here, and to impress upon him how powerless he was.

Powerless! A flicker of stubborn will stirred to respond to that implied challenge. All right, the mysterious *they* had made him do this. But they had underrated him by letting him learn, almost contemptuously, of their presence by that revelation. So warned, he was in a manner armed; he could prepare to fight back.

He squatted by the wreckage as he thought that through, turning over broken pieces. And, Shann realized, he must present at the moment a satisfactory picture of despondency to any spy. A spy, that was it! Someone or something must have him under observation, or his activities of the day before would not have been so summarily countered. And if there was a spy, then there was his answer to the riddle. To trap the trapper. Such action might be a project beyond his resources, but it was his own counterattack.

So now he had to play a role. Not only must he search the island for the trace of his spy, but he must do it in such a fashion that his purpose would not be plain to the enemy he suspected. The wolverines could help. Shann arose, allowed his shoulders to droop, slouching to the slope with all the air of a beaten man which he could assume, whistling for Taggi and Togi.

When they came, his exploration began. Ostensibly he

was hunting for lengths of drift or suitable growing saplings to take the place of those he had destroyed under orders. But he kept a careful watch on the animal pair, hoping by their reactions to pick up a clue to any hidden watcher.

The larger of the two beaches marked the point where the Terrans had first landed and where the shell thing had been killed. The smaller was more of a narrow tongue thrust out into the lagoon, much of it choked with sizable boulders. On earlier visits there Taggi and Togi had poked into the hollows among these with their usual curiosity. But now both animals remained upslope, showing no inclination to descend to the water line.

Shann caught hold of Taggi's scruff, pulling him along. The wolverine twisted and whined, but he did not fight for freedom as he would have upon scenting Throg. Not that the Terran had ever believed one of those aliens was responsible for the happenings on the island.

Taggi came down under Shann's urging, but he was plainly ill at ease. And at last he snarled a warning when the man would have drawn him closer to two rocks which met overhead in a crude semblance of an arch. There was a stick of drift protruding from that hollow affording Shann a legitimate excuse to venture closer. He dropped his hold on the wolverines, stooped to gather in the length of wood, and at the same time glanced into the pocket.

Water lay just beyond, making this a doorway to the lagoon. The sun had not yet penetrated into the shadow, if it ever did. Shann reached for the wood, at the same time drawing his finger across the flat rock which would furnish a steppingstone for anything using that door as an entrance to the island.

Wet! Which might mean his visitor had recently arrived, or else merely that a splotch of spray had landed there not too long before. But in his mind Shann was convinced that he had found the spy's entrance. Could he turn it into a trap? He added a piece of drift to his bundle and picked up two more before he returned to the cliff ahead.

A trap . . . He revolved in his mind all the traps he knew which could be used here. He already had decided upon the bait—his own work. And if his plans went through—and hope does not die easily—then this time he would not waste his labor either.

So he went back to the same job he had done the day before, making do with skin strips he had considered second-best before, smoothing, cutting. Only the trap occupied his mind, and close to sunset he knew just what he was going to do and how.

Though the Terran did not know the nature of the unseen opponent, he thought he could guess two weaknesses which might deliver the other into his hands. First, the enemy was entirely confident of success in this venture. No being who was able to control Shann as completely and ably as had been done the night before would credit any prey with the power to strike back in force.

Second, such a confident enemy would be unable to resist watching the manipulation of a captive. The Terran was certain that his opponent would be on the scene somewhere when he was led, dreaming, to destroy his work once more.

He might be wrong on both of those counts, but inwardly he didn't believe so. However, he had to wait until the dark to set up his own answer, one so simple he was certain the enemy would not suspect it at all.

11. THE WITCH

THERE were patches of light in the inner valley marking the phosphorescent plants, some creeping at ground level, others tall as saplings. On other nights Shann had welcomed that wan radiance, but now he lay in as relaxed a position as possible, marking each of those potential betrayers as he tried to counterfeit the attitude of sleep and at the same time plan out his route.

He had purposely settled in a pool of shadow, the wolverines beside him. And he thought that the bulk of the animal's bodies would cover his own withdrawal when the time came to move. One arm lying limply across his middle was in reality clutching to him an intricate arrangement of small hide straps which he had made by sacrificing most of the remainder of his painfully acquired thongs. The trap must be set in place soon!

Now that he had charted a path to the crucial point avoiding all light plants, Shann was ready to move. The Terran pressed his hand on Taggi's head in the one imperative command the wolverine was apt to obey—the order to stay where he was.

Shann sat up and gave the same voiceless instruction to Togi. Then he inched out of the hollow, a worm's progress to that narrow way along the cliff top—the path which anyone or anything coming up from that sea gate on the beach would have to pass in order to witness the shoreline occupied by the half-built outrigger.

111

So much of his plan was based upon luck and guesses, but those were all Shann had. And as he worked at the stretching of his snare, the Terran's heart pounded, and he tensed at every sound out of the night. Having tested all the anchoring of his net, he tugged at a last knot, and then crouched to listen not only with his ears, but with all his strength of mind and body.

Pound of waves, whistle of wind, the sleepy complaint of some bird . . . A regular splashing! One of the fish in the lagoon? Or what he awaited? The Terran retreated as noiselessly as he had come, heading for the hollow where he had bedded down.

He reached there breathless, his heart pumping, his mouth dry as if he had been racing. Taggi stirred and thrust a nose inquiringly against Shann's arm. But the wolverine made no sound, as if he, too, realized that some menace lay beyond the rim of the valley. Would that other come up the path Shann had trapped? Or had he been wrong? Was the enemy already stalking him from the other beach? The grip of his stunner was slippery in his damp hand; he hated this waiting.

The canoe . . . his work on it had been a careless botching. Better to have the job done right. Why, it was perfectly clear now how he had been mistaken! His whole work plan was wrong; he could see the right way of doing things laid out as clear as a blueprint in his mind. A picture in his mind!

Shann stood up and both wolverines moved uneasily, though neither made a sound. A picture in his mind! But this time he wasn't asleep; he wasn't dreaming a dream— to be used for his own defeat. Only (that other could not know this) the pressure which had planted the idea of new work to be done in his mind—an idea one part of him accepted as fact—had not taken warning from his move. He was supposed to be under control; the Terran was sure of that. All right, so he would play that part. He must if he would entice the trapper into his trap.

He holstered his stunner, walked out into the open, paying no heed now to the patches of light through which he must pass on his way to the path his own feet had already worn to the boat beach. As he went, Shann tried to counterfeit what he believed would be the gait of a man under compulsion.

Now he was on the rim fronting the downslope, fighting against his desire to turn and see for himself if anything had climbed behind. The canoe was all wrong, a bad job which he must make better at once so that in the morning he would be free of this island prison.

The pressure of that other's will grew stronger. And the Terran read into that the overconfidence which he believed would be part of the enemy's character. The one who was sending him to destroy his own work had no suspicion that the victim was not entirely malleable, ready to be used as he himself would use a knife or a force ax. Shann strode steadily downslope. With a small spurt of fear he knew that in a way that unseen other was right; the pressure was taking over, even though he was awake this time. The Terran tried to will his hand to his stunner, but his fingers fell instead on the hilt of his knife. He drew the blade as panic seethed in his head, chilling him from within. He had underestimated the other's power . . .

And that panic flared into open fight, making him forget his careful plans. Now he *must* wrench free from this control. The knife was moving to slash a hide lashing, directed by his hand, but not his will.

A soundless gasp, a flash of dismay rocked him, but neither was his gasp nor his dismay. That pressure snapped off; he was free. But the other wasn't! Knife still in fist, Shann turned and ran upslope, his torch in his other hand. He could see a shape now writhing, fighting, outlined against a light bush. And, fearing that the stranger might win free and disappear, the Terran spotlighted the captive in the beam, reckless of Throg or enemy reinforcements.

The other crouched, plainly startled by the sudden burst of light. Shann stopped abruptly. He had not really built up any mental picture of what he had expected to find in his snare, but this prisoner was as weirdly alien to him as a Throg. The light on the torch was reflected off a skin which glittered as if scaled, glittered with the brilliance of jewels in bands and coils of color spreading from the throat down the chest, spiraling about upper arms, around waist and thighs, as if the stranger wore a treasure house of gems as part of a living body. Except for those patterned loops, coils, and bands, the body had no clothing, though a belt about the slender middle supported a pair of pouches and some odd implements held in loops.

Roughly the figure was more humanoid than the Throgs. The upper limbs were not too unlike Shann's arms, though the hands had four digits of equal length instead of five. But the features were nonhuman, closer to saurian in contour. It had large eyes, blazing yellow in the dazzle of the flash, with verticle slits of green for pupils. A nose united with the jaw to make a snout, and above the domed forehead a sharp V-point of raised spiky growth extended back and down until behind the shoulder blades it widened and expanded to resemble a pair of wings.

The captive no longer struggled, but sat quietly in the tangle of the snare Shann had set, watching the Terran steadily as if there were no difficulty in seeing through the brilliance of the beam to the man who held it. And, oddly enough, Shann experienced no repulsion toward its reptilian appearance as he had upon first sighting the beetle-Throg. On impulse he put down his torch on a rock and walked into the light to face squarely the thing out of the sea.

Still eying Shann, the captive raised one limb and gave an absent-minded tug to the belt it wore. Shann, noting that gesture, was struck by a wild surmise, leading him to study the prisoner more narrowly. Allowing for the alien structure of bone, the nonhuman skin; this creature was delicate, graceful, in its way beautiful, with a fragility of limb which backed up his suspicions Moved by no pressure from the other, but by his own will and sense of fitness, Shann stooped to cut the control line of his snare.

The captive continued to watch as Shann sheathed his blade and then held out his hand. Yellow eyes, never blinking since his initial appearance, regarded him, not with any trace of fear or dismay, but with a calm measurement which was curiosity based upon a strong belief in its own superiority. He did not know how he knew, but Shann was certain that the creature out of the sea was still entirely confident, that it made no fight because it did not conceive of any possible danger from him. And again, oddly enough, he was not irritated by this unconscious arrogance; rather he was intrigued and amused.

"Friends?" Shann used the basic galactic speech devised by Survey and the Free Traders, semantics which depended upon the proper inflection of voice and tone to project meaning when the words were foreign.

The other made no sound, and the Terran began to wonder if his captive had any audible form of speech. He withdrew a step or two then pulled at the snare, drawing the cords away from the creature's slender ankles. Rolling the thongs into a ball, he tossed the crude net back over his shoulder.

"Friends?" he repeated again, showing his empty hands, trying to give that one word the proper inflection, hoping the other could read his peaceful intent in his features if not by his speech.

In one lithe, flowing movement the alien arose. Fully erect, the Warlockian had a frail appearance. Shann, for his breed, was not tall. But the native was still smaller, not more than five feet, that stiff V of head crest just topping Shann's shoulder. Whether any of those fittings at its belt could be a weapon the Terran had no way of telling. However, the other made no move to draw any of them.

Instead, one of the four-digit hands came up. Shann felt the feather touch of strange finger tips on his chin, across his lips, up his cheek, to at last press firmly on his forehead at a spot just between the eyebrows. What followed was communication of a sort, not in words or in any describable flow of thoughts. There was no feeling of enmity—at least nothing strong enough to be called that. Curiosity, yes, and then a growing doubt, not of the Terran himself, but of the other's preconceived ideas concerning him. Shann was other than the native had judged him, and the stranger was disturbed, that self-confidence a little ruffled. And also Shann was right in his guess. He smiled, his amusement growing—not aimed at his companion on this cliff top, but at himself. For he was dealing with a woman, a very young woman, and someone as fully feminine in her way as any human girl could be.

"Friends?" he asked for the third time.

But the other still exuded a wariness, a wariness mixed with surprise. And the tenuous message which passed between them then astounded Shann. To this Warlockian out of the night he was not following the proper pattern of male behaviour at all; he should have been in awe of the other merely because of her sex. A diffidence rather

116

than an assumption of equality should have colored his response, judged by her standards. At first, he caught a flash of anger at this preposterous attitude of his; then her curiosity won, but there was still no reply to his question.

The finger tips no longer made contact between them. Stepping back, her hands now reached for one of the pouches at her belt. Shann watched that movement carefully. And because he did not trust her too far, he whistled.

Her head came up. She might be dumb, but plainly she was not deaf. And she gazed down into the hollow as the wolverines answered his summons with growls. Her profile reminded Shann of something for an instant; but it should have been golden-yellow instead of silver with two jeweled patterns ringing the snout. Yes, that small plaque he had seen in the cabin of one of the ship's officers. A very old Terran legend—"Dragon," the officer had named the creature. Only that one had possessed a serpent's body, a lizard's legs and wings.

Shann gave a sudden start, aware his thoughts had made him careless, or had she in some way led him into that bypath of memory for her own purposes? Because now she held some object in the curve of her curled fingers, regarding him with those unblinking yellow eyes. Eyes . . . eyes . . . Shann dimly heard the alarm cry of the wolverines. He tried to snap draw his stunner, but it was too late.

There was a haze about him hiding the rocks, the island valley with its radiant plants, the night sky, the bright beam of the torch. Now he moved through that haze as one walks through a dream approaching nightmare, striding with an effort as if wading through a deterring flood. Sound, sight—one after another those senses were taken from him. Desperately Shann held to one thing, his own sense of identity. He was Shann Lantee, Terran breed, out of Tyr, of the Survey Service. Some part of him repeated those facts with vast urgency against an almost overwhelming force which strove to defeat that awareness of self, making him nothing but a tool—or a weapon—for another's use.

The Terran fought, soundlessly but fiercely, on a battleground which was within him, knowing in a detached way that his body obeyed another's commands.

"I am Shann—" he cried without audible speech. "I am myself. I have two hands, two legs . . . I think for myself! I am a *man*—"

And to that came an answer of sorts, a blow of will striking at his resistance, a will which struggled to drown him before ebbing, leaving behind it a faint suggestion of bewilderment, of a dawn of concern.

"I am a *man!*" he hurled that assertion as he might have thrust deep with one of the crude spears he had used against the Throgs. For against what he faced now his weapons were as crude as spears fronting blasters. "I am Shann Lantee, Terran, man . . ." Those were facts; no haze could sweep them from his mind or take away that heritage.

And again there was the lightening of the pressure, the slight recoil, which could only be a prelude to another assault upon his last stronghold. He clutched his three facts to him as a shield, groping for others which might have afforded a weapon of rebuttal.

Dreams, these Warlockians dealt in and through dreams. And the opposite of dreams are facts! His name, his breed, his sex—these were facts. And Warlock itself was a fact. The earth under his boots was a fact. The water which washed around the island was a fact. The air he breathed was a fact. Flesh, blood, bones—facts, all of them. Now he was a struggling identity imprisoned in a rebel body. But that body was real. He tried to feel it. Blood pumped from his heart, his lungs filled and emptied; he struggled to feel those processes.

With a terrifying shock, the envelope which had held him vanished. Shann was choking, struggling in water. He flailed out with his arms, kicked his legs. One hand grated painfully against stone. Hardly knowing what he did, but fighting for his life, Shann caught at that rock and drew his head out of water. Coughing and gasping, half drowned, he was weak with the panic of his close brush with death.

For a long moment he could only cling to the rock which had saved him, retching and dazed, as the water washed about his body, a current tugging at his trailing legs. There was light of a sort here, patches of green which glowed with the same subdued light as the bushes of the outer world, for he was no longer under the night sky. A rock-roof was but inches over his head; he must be in some cave or tunnel under the surface of the sea. Again a gust of panic shook him as he felt trapped.

The water continued to pull at Shann, and in his weakened condition it was a temptation to yield to that pull; the more he fought it the more he was exhausted. At last the Terran turned on his back, trying to float with the stream, sure he could no longer battle it.

Luckily those few inches of space above the surface of the water continued, and he had air to breathe. But the fear of that ending, of being swept under the surface, chewed at his nerves. And his bodily danger burned away the last of the spell which had held him, brought him into this place, wherever it might be.

Was it only his heightened imagination, or had the current grown swifter? Shann tried to gauge the speed of his passage by the way the patches of green light slipped by. Now he turned and began to swim slowly, feeling as

119

if his arms were leaden weights, his ribs a cage to bind his aching lungs.

Another patch of light . . . larger . . . spreading across the roof over head. Then, he was out! Out of the tunnel into a cavern so vast that its arching roof was like a skydome far above his head. But here the patches of light were brighter, and they were arranged in odd groups which had a familiar look to them.

Only, better than freedom overhead, there was a shore not too distant. Shann swam for that haven, summoning up the last rags of his strength, knowing that if he could not reach it very soon he was finished. Somehow he made it and lay gasping, his cheek resting on sand finer than any of the outer world, his fingers digging into it for purchase to drag his body on. But when he collapsed, his legs were still awash in water.

No footfall could be heard on that sand. But he knew that he was no longer alone. He braced his hands and with painful effort levered up his body. Somehow he made it to his knees, but he could not stand. Instead he half tumbled back, so that he faced them from a sitting position.

Them—there were three of them—the dragon-headed ones with their slender, jewel-set bodies glittering even in this subdued light, their yellow eyes fastened on him with a remoteness which did not approach any human emotion, save perhaps that of a cold and limited wonder. But behind them came a fourth, one he knew by the patterns on her body.

Shann clasped his hands about his knees to still the trembling of his body, and eyed them back with all the defiance he could muster. Nor did he doubt that he had been brought here, his body as captive to their will, as had been that of their spy or messenger in his crude snare on the island.

"Well, you have me," he said hoarsely. "Now what?"

His words boomed weirdly out over the water, were echoed from the dim outer reaches of the cavern. There was no answer. They merely stood watching him. Shann stiffened, determined to hold to his defiance and to that identity which he now knew was his weapon against the powers they used.

The one who had somehow drawn him there moved at last, circling around the other three with a suggestion of diffidence in her manner. Shann jerked back his head as her hand stretched to touch his face. And then, guessing that she sought her peculiar form of communication, he submitted to her finger tips, though now his skin crawled under that light but firm pressure and he shrank from the contact.

There were no sensations this time. To his amazement a concrete inquiry shaped itself in his brain, as clear as if the question had been asked aloud: "Who are you?"

"Shann . . ." he began vocally, and then turned words into thoughts. "Shann Lantee, Terran, man." He made his answer the same which had kept him from succumbing to their complete domination.

"Name—Shann Lantee, man—yes." The other accepted those. "Terran?" That was a question.

Did these people have any notion of space travel? Could they understand the concept of another world holding intelligent beings?

"I come from another world . . ." He tried to make a cleancut picture in his mind—a globe in space, a ship blasting free . . .

"Look!" The fingers still rested between his eyebrows, but with her other hand the Warlockian was pointing up to the dome of the cavern.

Shann followed her order. He studied those patches of light which had seemed so vaguely familiar at his first sighting, studying them closely to know them for what they were. A star map! A map of the heavens as they could be seen from the outer crust of Warlock.

"Yes, I come from the stars," he answered, booming with his voice.

The fingers dropped from his forehead; the scaled head swung around to exchange glances, which were perhaps some unheard communication with the other three. Then the hand was extended again.

"Come!"

Fingers fell from his head to his right wrist, closing there with surprising strength; and some of that strength together with a new energy flowed from them into him, so that he found and kept his feet as the other drew him up.

12. THE VEIL OF ILLUSION

Perhaps his status was that of a prisoner, but Shann was too tired to press for an explanation. He was content to be left alone in the unusual circular, but roofless, room of the structure to which they had brought him. There was a thick matlike pallet in one corner, short for the length of his body, but softer than any bed he had rested on since he had left the Terran camp before the coming of the Throgs. Above him glimmered those patches of light symbolizing the lost stars. He blinked at them until they all ran together in bands like the jeweled coils on Warlockian bodies; then he slept—dreamlessly.

The Terran awoke with all his senses alert; some silent alarm might have triggered that instant awareness of himself and his surroundings. There had been no change in the star pattern still overhead; no one had entered the round chamber. Shann rolled over on his mat bed, conscious that all his aches had vanished. Just as his mind was clearly active, so did his body also respond effortlessly to his demands. He was not aware of any hunger or thirst, though a considerable length of time must have passed since he had made his mysteriously contrived exit from the outer world.

In spite of the humidity of the air, his ragged garments had dried on his body. Shann got to his feet, trying to order the sorry remnants of his uniform, eager to be on the move. Though to where and for what purpose he could not have answered.

The door through which he had entered remained closed, refusing to yield to his push. Shann stepped back, eyeing the distance to the top of the partition between the roofless rooms. The walls were smooth with the gloss of a sea shell's interior, but the exuberant confidence which had been with him since his awakening refused to accept such a minor obstacle.

He made two test leaps, both times his fingers striking the wall well below the top of the partition. Shann gathered himself together as might a cat and tried the third time, putting into that effort every last ouce of strength, determination and will. He made it, though his arms jerked as the weight of his body hung from his hands. Then a scramble, a knee hooked over the top, and he was perched on the wall, able to study the rest of the building.

In shape, the structure was unlike anything he had seen on his home world or reproduced in any of the tri-dee records of Survey accessible to him. The rooms were either circular or oval, each separated from the next by a short passage, so that the overall impression was that of ten strings of beads radiating from a central knot of one large chamber, all with the uniform nacre walls and a limited amount of furnishings.

As he balanced on the narrow perch, Shann could sight no other movement in the nearest line of rooms, those connected by corridors with his own. He got to his feet to walk the tightrope of the upper walls toward that inner chamber which was the heart of the Warlockian— palace? town apartment dwelling? At least it was the only structure on the island, for he could see the outer rim of that smooth soft sand ringing it about. The island itself was curiously symmetrical, a perfect oval, too perfect to be a natural outcrop of sand and rock.

There was no day or night here in the cavern. The light from the roof patches remained constantly the same, and that flow was abetted within the building by a soft radiation from the walls. Shann reached the next room in line, hunkering down to see within it. To all appearances the chamber was exactly the same as the one he had just left; there were the same unadorned walls, a thick mat bed against the far side, and no indication whether it was in use or had not been entered for days.

He was on the next section of corridor wall when he caught that faint taint in the air, the very familiar scent of wolverines. Now it provided Shann with a guide as well as a promise of allies.

The next bead-room gave him what he wanted. Below him Taggi and Togi paced back and forth. They had already torn to bits the sleeping mat which had been the chamber's single furnishing, and their temper was none too certain. As Shann squatted well above their range of vision, Taggi reared against the opposite wall, his claws finding no hold on the smooth coating of its surface. They were as competently imprisoned as if they had been dropped into a huge fishbowl, and they were not taking to it kindly.

124

How had the animals been brought here? Down that water tunnel by the same unknown method he himself had been transported until that almost disastrous awakening in the center of the flood? The Terran did not doubt that the doors of the room were as securely fastened as those of his own further down the corridor. For the moment the wolverines were safe; he could not free them. And he was growing increasingly certain that if he found any of his native jailers, it would be at the center of that wheel of rooms and corridors.

Shann made no attempt to attract the animals' attention, but kept on along his tightrope path. He passed two more rooms, both empty, both differing in no way from those he had already inspected; and then he came to the central chamber, four times as big as any of the rest and with a much brighter wall light.

The Terran crouched, one hand on the surface of the partition top as an additional balance, the other gripping his stunner. For some reason his captors had not disarmed him. Perhaps they believed they had no necessity to fear his off-world weapon.

"Have you grown wings?"

The words formed in his brain, bringing with them a sense on calm amusement to reduce all his bold exploration to the level of a child's first staggering steps. Shann fought his first answering flare of pure irritation. To lose even a fraction of control was to open a door for them. He remained where he was as if he had never "heard" that question, surveying the room below with all the impassiveness he could summon.

Here the walls were no smooth barrier, but honeycombed with niches in a regular pattern. And in each of the niches rested a polished skull, a nonhuman skull. Only the outlines of those ranked bones were familiar; for just so had looked the great purple-red rock where the wheeling flyers issued from the eye sockets. A rock island had been fashioned into a skull—by design or nature?

And upon closer observation the Terran could see that there was a difference among these ranked skulls, a mutation of coloring from row to row, a softening of outline, perhaps by the wearing of time.

There was also a table of dull black, rising from the flooring on legs which were not more than a very few inches high, so that from his present perch the board appeared to rest on the pavement itself. Behind the table in a row, as shopkeepers might await a customer, three of the Warlockians, seated cross-legged on mats, their hands folded primly before them. And at the side a fourth, the one whom he had trapped on the island.

Not one of those spiked heads rose to view him. But they knew that he was there; perhaps they had known the very instant he had left the room or cell in which they had shut him. And they were so very sure of themselves . . . Once again Shann subdued a spark of anger. That same patience with its core of stubborn determination which had brought him to Warlock backed his moves now. The Terran swung down, landing lightly on his feet, facing the three behind the table, towering well over them as he stood erect, yet gaining no sense of satisfaction from that merely physical fact.

"You have come." The words sounded as if they might be a part of some polite formula. So he replied in kind and aloud.

"I have come." Without waiting for their bidding, he dropped into the same cross-legged pose, fronting them now on a more equal level across their dead black table.

"And why have you come, star voyager?" That thought seemed to be a concentrated effort from all three rather than any individual questioning.

126

"And why did you bring me?" He hesitated, trying to think of some polite form of address. Those he knew which were appropriate to their sex on other worlds seemed incongruous when applied to the bizarre figures now facing him. "Wise ones," he finally chose.

Those unblinking yellow eyes conveyed no emotion; certainly his human gaze could detect no change of expression on their nonhuman faces.

"You are a male."

"I am," he agreed, not seeing just what that fact had to do with either diplomatic fencing or his experiences of the immediate past.

"Where then is your thoughtguider?"

Shann puzzled over that conception, guessed at its meaning.

"I am my own thoughtguider," he returned stoutly, with all the conviction he could manage to put into that reply.

Again he met a yellow-green stare, but he sensed a change in them. Some of their complacency had ebbed; his reply had been as a stone dropped into a quiet pool, sending ripples out afar to disturb the customary mirror surface of smooth serenity.

"The star-born one speaks the truth!" That came from the Warlockian who had been his fist contact.

"It would appear that he does." The agreement was measured, and Shann knew that he was meant to "overhear" that.

"It would seem, Readers-of-the-rods"—the middle one of the triumvirate at the table spoke now—"that all living things do not follow our pattern of life. But that is possible. A male who thinks for himself . . . unguided, who dreams perhaps! Or who can understand the truth of dreaming! Strange indeed must be his people. Sharers-of-my-visions, let us consult the Old Ones concerning this."

For the first time one of those crested heads moved, the gaze shifted from Shann to the ranks of the skulls, pausing at one.

Shann, ready for any wonder, did not betray his amazement when the ivory inhabitant of that particular niche moved, lifted from its small compartment, and drifted buoyantly through the air to settle at the right-hand corner of the table. Only when it had safely grounded did the eyes of the Warlockian move to another niche on the other side of the curving room, this time bringing up from close to floor level a time-darkened skull to occupy the left corner of the table.

There was a third shifting from the weird storehouse, a last skull to place between the other two. And now the youngest native arose from her mat to bring a bowl of green crystal. One of her seniors took it in both hands, making a gesture of offering it to all three skulls, and then gazed over its rim at the Terran.

"We shall cast the rods, man-who-thinks-without-a-guide. Perhaps then we shall see how strong *your* dreams are—to be bent to your using, or to break you for your impudence."

Her hands swayed the bowl from side to side, and there was an answering whisper from its interior as if the contents slid loosely there. Then one of her companions reached forward and gave a quick tap to the bottom of that container, spilling out upon the table a shower of brightly colored slivers each an inch or so long.

Shann, staring at the display in bewilderment, saw that in spite of the seeming carelessness of that toss the small needles had spread out on the blank surface to form a design in arrangement and color. And he wondered how that skillfull trick had been accomplished.

All three of the Warlockians bent their heads to study the grouping of the tiny sticks, their young subordinate leaning forward also, her eagerness less well controlled than her elders'. And now it was as if a curtain had fallen between the Terran and the aliens, all sense of communication which had been with him since he had entered the skull-lined chamber was summarily cut off.

A hand moved, making the jeweled pattern—braceleting wrist and extending up the arm—flash subdued fire. Fingers swept the sticks back into the bowl; four pairs of yellow eyes raised to regard Shann once more, but the blanket of their withdrawal still held.

The youngest Warlockian took the bowl from the elder who held it, stood for a long moment with it resting between her palms, fixing Shann with an unreadable stare. Then she came toward him. One of those at the table put out a restraining hand.

This time Shann did *not* master his start as he heard the first audible voice which had not been his own. The skull at the left hand on the table, by its yellowed color the oldest of those summoned from the niches, was moving, moving because its jaws gaped and then snapped, emitting a faint bleat which might have been a word or two.

She who would have halted the young Warlockian's advance, withdrew her hand. Then her fingers curled in an unmistakable beckoning gesture. Shann came to the table, but he could not quite force himself near that chattering skull, even though it had stopped its jig of speech.

The bowl of sticks was offered to him. Still no message from mind to mind, but he could guess at what they wanted of him. The crystal substance was not cool to the touch as he had expected; rather it was warm, as living flesh might feel. And the colored sticks filled about two thirds of the interior, lying all mixed together without any order.

Shann concentrated on recalling the ceremoney the

Warlockian had used before the first toss. She had offered the bowl to the skulls in turn. The skulls! But he was no consulter of skulls. Still holding the bowl close to his chest, Shann looked up over the roofless walls at the star map on the roof of the cavern. There, that was Rama; and to its left, just a little above, was Tyr's system where swung the stark world of his birth, and of which he had only few good memories, but of which he was a part. The Terran raised the bowl to that spot of light which marked Tyr's pale sun.

Smiling with a wry twist, he lowered the bowl, and on impulse of pure defiance he offered it to the skull that had chattered. Immediately he realized that the move had had an electric effect upon the aliens. Slowly at first, and then faster, he began to swing the bowl from side to side, the needles slipping, mixing within. And as he swung it, Shann held it out over the expanse of the table.

The Warlockian who had given him the bowl was the one who struck it on the bottom, causing a rain of splinters. To Shann's astonishment, mixed as they had been in the container, they once more formed a pattern, and not the same pattern the Warlockians had consulted earlier. The dampening curtain between them vanished; he was in touch mind to mind once again.

"So be it." The center Warlockian spread out her four-fingered thumbless hands above the scattered needles. "What is read, is read."

Again a formula. He caught a chorus of answer from the others.

"What is read, is read. To the dreamer the dream. Let the dream be known for what it is, and there is life. Let the dream encompass the dreamer falsely, and all is lost."

"Who can question the wisdom of the Old Ones?" asked their leader. "We are those who read the messages they send, out of their mercy. This is a strange thing they bid us do, man—open for you our own initiates' road to the veil of illusion. That way has never been for males, who dream without set purpose and have not the ability to know true from false, have not the courage to face their dreams to the truth. Do so—if you can!" There was a flash of mockery in that; combined with something else —stronger than distaste, not as strong as hatred, but certainly not friendly.

She held out her hands and Shann saw now, lying on a slowly closing palm, a disk such as the one Thorvald had shown him. The Terran had only one moment of fear and then came blackness, more absolute than the dark of any night he had ever known.

Light once more, green light with an odd shimmering quality to it. The skull-lined walls were gone; there were no walls, no building held him. Shann strode forward, and his boots sank in sand, that smooth, satin sand which had ringed the island in the cavern. But he was certain he was no longer on that island, even within that cavern, though far above him there was still a dome of roof.

The source of the green shimmer lay to his left. Somehow he found himself reluctant to turn and face it. That would commit him to action. But Shann turned.

A veil, a veil or rippling green. Material? No, rather mist or light. A veil depending from some source so far over his head that its origin was hidden in the upper gloom, a veil which was a barrier he must cross.

With every nerve protesting, Shann walked forward, unable to keep back. He flung up his arm to protect his face as he marched into that stuff. It was warm, and the gas—if gas it was—left no slick of moisture on his skin in spite of its foggy consistency. And it was no veil or curtain, for although he was already well into the murk, he saw no end to it. Blindly he trudged on, unable to sight anything but the rolling billows of green, pausing now and again to go down on one knee and pat the sand underfoot, reassured at the reality of that footing.

And when he met nothing menacing, Shann began to relax. His heart no longer labored; he made no move to draw the stunner or knife. Where he was and for what purpose, he had no idea. But there *was* a purpose in this and that the Warlockians were behind it, he did not doubt. The "initiates' road," the leader had said, and the conviction was steady in his mind that he faced some test of alien devising.

A cavern with a green veil—his memory awoke. Thorvald's dream! Shann paused, trying to remember how the other had described this place. So he was enacting Thorvald's dream! And could the Survey officer now be caught in Shann's dream in turn, climbing up somewhere into the nose slit of a skull-shaped mountain?

Green fog without end, and Shann lost in it. How long had he been here? Shann tried to reckon time, the time since his coming into the water-world of the starred cavern. He realized that he had not eaten, nor drank, nor desired to do so either—nor did he now. Yet he was not weak; in fact, he had never felt such tireless energy as possessed his spare body.

Was this *all* a dream? His threatened drowning in the underground stream a nightmare? Yet there was a pattern in this, just as there had been a pattern in the needles he had spilled across the table. One even led to another with discernible logic; because he had tossed that particular pattern he had come here.

According to the ambiguous instructions or warnings of the Warlockian witch, his safety in this place would depend upon his ability to tell true dreams from false. But how . . . why? So far he had done nothing except walk through a green fog, and for all he knew, he might well be traveling in circles.

Because there was nothing else to do, Shann walked on, his boots pressing sand, rising from each step with a small sucking sound. Then, as he stooped to search for some indication of a path or road which might guide him, his ears caught the slightest of noises—other small sucking whispers. He was not the only wayfarer in this place!

13. HE WHO DREAMS . . .

THE MIST was not a quiet thing; it billowed and curled until it appeared to half-conceal darker shadows, any one of which could be an enemy. Shann remained hunkered on the sand, every sense abnormally alert, watching the fog. He was still sure he could hear sounds which marked the progress of another. What other? One of the War-lockians tracking him to spy? Or was there some prisoner like himself lost out there in the murk? Could it be Thorvald?

Now the sound had ceased. He was not even sure from what direction it had first come. Perhaps that other was listening now, as intent upon locating him. Shann ran his tongue over dry lips. The impulse to call out, to try and contact any fellow traveler here, was strong. Only hard-learned caution kept him silent. He got to his hands and knees, uncertain as to his previous direction.

Shann crept. Someone expecting a man walking erect might be suitably distracted by the arrival of a half-seen figure on all fours. He halted again to listen.

He had been right! The sound of a very muffled foot-fall or footfalls, carried to his ears. He was sure that the sound was louder, that the unknown was approaching. Shann stood, his hand close to his stunner. He was almost tempted to spray that beam blindly before him, hoping to hit the unseen by chance.

A shadow—something more swift than a shadow, more than one of the tricks the curling fog played on eyes—was moving with purpose and straight for him. Still, prudence restrained Shann from calling out.

The figure grew clearer. A Terran! It could be Thorvald! But remembering how they had last parted, Shann did not hurry to meet him.

That shadow-shape stretched out a long arm in a sweep as if to pull aside some of the vapor concealing them from each other. Then Shann shivered as if that fog had suddenly turned into the drive of frigid snow. For the mist did roll back so that the two of them stood in an irregular clearing in its midst.

And he did not front Thorvald.

Shann was caught up in the ice grip of an old fear, frozen by it, but somehow clinging to a hope that he did not see the unbelievable.

Those hands drawing the lash of a whip back into striking readiness . . . a brutal nose broken askew, a blaster burn puckering across cheek to misshapen ear . . . that, evil, gloating grin of anticipation. Flick, flick, the slight dance of the lash in a master's hand as those thick fingers tightened about the stock of the whip. In a moment it would whirl up to lay a ribbon of fire about Shann's defenceless shoulders. Then Logally would laugh and laugh, his sadistic mirth echoed by those other men who played jackals to his rogue lion.

Other men . . . Shann shook his head dazedly. But he did not stand again in the Dump-size bar of the Big Strike. And he was no longer a terrorized youngster, fit meat for Logally's amusement. Only the whip rose, the ash curled out, catching Shann just as it had that time years ago, delivering a red slash of pure agony. But Logally was dead, Shann's mind screamed, fighting frantically against the evidence of his eyes, of that pain in his chest and shoulder. The Dump bully had been spaced by off-world miners, now also dead, whose claims he had tried to jump out in the Ajax system.

Logally drew back the lash, preparing to strike again. Shann faced a man five years dead who walked and fought. Or, Shann bit hard upon his lower lip, holding desperately to sane reasoning—did he indeed face anything? Logally was the ancient devil of his boyhood, produced anew by the witchery of Warlock. Or had Shann himself been led to recreate both the man and the circumstances of their first meeting with fear as a weapon to pull the creator down? Dream true or false. Logally *was* dead; therefore, this dream was false, it had to be.

The Terran began to walk toward that grinning ogre rising out of his old nightmares. His hand was no longer on the butt of his stunner, but swung loosely at his side. He saw the coming lash, the wicked promise in those small narrowed eyes. This was Logally at the acme of his strength, when he was most to be feared, as he had continued to exist over the years in the depths of a boy-child's memory. But Logally was *not* alive; only in a dream could he be.

For the second time the lash bit at Shann, curling about his body, to dissolve. There was no alteration in Logally's grin. His muscular arm drew back as he aimed a third blow. Shann continued to walk forward, bringing up one hand, not to strike at that sweating, bristly jaw, but as if to push the other out of his path. And in his mind he held one thought: this was not Logally; it could not be. Ten years had passed since they had met. And for five of those years Logally had been dead. Here was

Warlockian witchery, to be met by sane Terran reasoning.

Shann was alone. The mist, which had formed walls
enclosed him again. But still there was a smarting brand
across his shoulder. Shann drew aside the rags of his
uniform blouse to discover a welt, raw and red. And
seeing that, his unbelief was shaken.

When he had believed in Logally and in Logally's
weapon, the other had had reality enough to strike that
blow, make the lash cut deep. But when the Terran had
faced the phantom with the truth, then neither Logally
nor his lash existed. Shann shivered, trying not to think
what might lie before him. Visions out of nightmare
which could put on substance! He had dreamed of
Logally in the past, many times. And he had had other
dreams, just as frightening. Must he front those nightmares, all of them—? Why? To amuse his captors, or to
prove their contention that he was a fool to challenge the
powers of such mistresses of illusion?

How did they know just what dreams to use in order to
break him? Or did he himself furnish the actors and the
action, projecting old terrors in this mist as a tri-dee tape
projected a story in three dimensions for the amusement
of the viewer?

Dream true—was this progress through the mist also a
dream? Dreams within dreams . . . Shann put his hand to
his head, uncertain, badly shaken. But that stubborn core
of determination within him was still holding. Next time
he would be prepared at once to face down any resur-
rected memory.

Walking slowly, pausing to listen for the slightest
sound which might herald the coming of a new illusion,
Shann tried to guess which of his nightmares might come
to face him. But he was to learn that there was more than

ne kind of dream. Steeled against old fears, he was met
y another emotion altogether.

There was a fluttering in the air, a little crooning cry
vhich pulled at his heart. Without any conscious thought,
hann held out his hands, whistling on two notes a call
vhich his lips appeared to remember more quickly than
is mind. The shape which winged through the fog came
traight to his waiting hold, tore at long-walled-away
urt with its once familiar beauty. It flew with a list; one
f the delicately tinted wings was injured, had never
eeled straight. But the seraph nestled into the hollow
f Shann's two palms and looked up at him with all the
ld liquid trust.

"Trav! Trav!" He cradled the tiny creature carefully,
egarded with joy its feathered body, the curled plumes
n its proudly held head, felt the silken patting of those
nfinitesimal claws against his protecting fingers.

Shann sat down in the sand, hardly daring to breathe.
rav—again! The wonder of this never-to-be-hoped-for
eturn filled him with a surge of happiness almost too
reat to bear, which hurt in its way with as great a pain
s Logally's lash; it was a pain rooted in love, not fear
nd hate.

Logally's lash . . .

Shann trembled. Trav raised one of those small claws
oward the Terran's face, crooning a soft caressing cry for
ecognition, for protection, trying to be a part of Shann's
ife once more.

Trav! How could he bear to will Trav into nothingness,
o bear to summon up another harsh memory which
vould sweep Trav away? Trav was the only thing Shann
ad ever known which he could love wholeheartedly,
hat had answered his love with a return gift of affection
o much greater than the light body he now held.

"Trav!" he whispered softly. Then he made his great effort again this second and far more subtle attack. With the same agony which he had known years earlier, he resolutely summoned a bitter memory, sat nursing once more a broken thing which died in pain he could not ease, aware himself of every moment of that pain. And what was worse, this time there clung that nagging little doubt. What if he had not forced the memory? Perhaps he could have taken Trav with him unhurt, alive, at least for a while.

Shann covered his face with his now empty hands. To see a nightmare flicker out after facing squarely up to its terror, that was no great task. To give up a dream which was part of a lost heaven, that cut cruelly deep. The Terran dragged himself to his feet, drained and weary, stumbling on.

Was there no end to this aimless circling through a world of green smoke? He shambled ahead, moving his feet leadenly. How long had he been here? There was no division in time, just the unchanging light which was a part of the fog through which he plodded.

Then he heard more than any shuffle of foot across sand, any crooning of a long dead seraph, the rising and falling of a voice: a human voice—not quite singing or reciting, but something between the two. Shann paused, searching his memory, a memory which seemed bruised, for the proper answer to match that sound.

But, though he recalled scene after scene out of the years, that voice did not trigger any return from his past. He turned toward its source, dully determined to get over quickly the meeting which lay behind that signal. Only, though he walked on and on, Shann did not appear any closer to the man behind the voice, nor was he able to make out separate words composing that chant, a chant broken now and then by pauses, so that the Terran

138

grew aware of the distress of his fellow prisoner. For the impression that he sought another captive came out of nowhere and grew as he cast wider and wider in his quest.

Then he might have turned some invisible corner in the midst, for the chant broke out anew in stronger volume, and now he was able to distinguish words he knew.

"... where blow the winds between the worlds,
And hang the suns in dark of space.
For Power is given a man to use.
Let him do so well before the last accounting—"

The voice was hoarse, cracked, the words spaced with uneven catches of breath, as if they had been repeated many, many times to provide an anchor against madness, form a tie to reality. And hearing that note, Shann slowed his pace. This was out of no memory of his; he was sure of that.

"... blow the winds between the worlds,
And hang the suns in ... dark—of—of—"

That harsh croak of voice was running down, as a clock runs down for lack of winding. Shann sped on, reacting to a plea which did not lay in the words themselves.

Once more the mist curled back, provided him with an open space. A man sat on the sand, his fists buried wrist deep in the smooth grains on either side of his body, his eyes set, red-rimmed, glazed, his body rocking back and forth in time to his labored chant.

"... the dark of space—"

"Thorvald!" Shann skidded in the sand, went down on his knees. The manner of their last parting was forgotten as he took in the officer's condition.

The other did not stop his swaying, but his head

turned with a stiff jerk, the gray eyes making a visible effort to focus on Shann. Then some of the strain smoothed out of the gaunt features and Thorvald laughed softly.

"Garth!"

Shann stiffened but had no chance to protest that mistaken identification as the other continued: "So you made class one status, boy! I always knew you could if you'd work for it. A couple of black marks on your record, sure. But those can be rubbed out, boy, when you're willing to try. Thorvalds always have been Survey. Our father would have been proud."

Thorvald's voice flattened, his smile faded, there was a growing spark of some emotion in those gray eyes. Unexpectedly, he hurled himself forward, his hands clawing for Shann's throat. He bore the younger man down under him to the sand where Lantee found himself fighting desperately for his life against a man who could only be mad.

Shann used a trick learned on the Dumps, and his opponent doubled up with a gasp of agony to let the younger man break free. He planted a knee on the small of Thorvald's back, digging the officer into the sand, pinning down his arms in spite of the other's struggles. Regaining his own breath in gulps, Shann tried to appeal to some spark of reason in the other.

"Thorvald! This is Lantee—Lantee—" His name echoed in the mist-walled void like an unhuman wail.

"Lantee—? No, Throg! Lantee—Throg—killed my brother!"

Sand puffed out with the breath which expelled that indictment. But Thorvald no longer fought, and Shann believed him close to collapse.

Shann relaxed his hold, rolling the other man over. Thorvald obeyed his pull limply, lying face upward, sand in his hair and eyebrows, crusting his slack lips. The younger man brushed the dirt away gently as the other opened his eyes to regard Shann with his old impersonal stare.

"You're alive," Thorvald stated bleakly. "Garth's dead. You ought to be dead too."

Shann drew back, rubbed sand from his hands, his concern dampened by the other's patent hostility. Only that angry accusation vanished in a blink of those gray eyes. Then there was a warmer recognition in Thorvald's expression.

"Lantee!" The younger man might just have come into sight. "What are you doing here?"

Shann tightened his belt. "Just about what you are." He was still aloof, giving no acknowledgment of difference in rank now. "Running around in this fog hunting the way out."

Thorvald sat up, surveying the billowing walls of the hole which contained them. Then he reached out a hand to draw fingers down Shann's forearm.

"You *are* real," he observed simply, and his voice was warm, welcoming.

"Don't bet on it," Shann snapped. "The unreal can be mighty real—here." His hand went up to the smarting brand on his shoulder.

Thorvald nodded. "Masters of illusion," he murmured.

"Mistresses," Shann corrected. "This place is run by a gang of pretty smart witches."

"Witches? You've seen them? Where? And what—who are they?" Thorvald pounced with a return of his old-time sharpness.

"They're females right enough, and they can make the impossible happen. I'd say that classifies them as witches. One of them tried to take me over back on the island. I set a trap and caught her; then somehow she transported me—" Swiftly he outlined the chain of events leading from his sudden awakening in the river tunnel to his present penetration of this fog-world.

Thorvald listened eagerly. When the story was finished, he rubbed his hands across his drawn face, smearing away the last of the sand. "At least you have some idea of who they are and a suggestion of how you got here. I don't remember that much about my own arrival. As far as I can remember I went to sleep on the island and woke up here!"

Shann studied him and knew that Thorvald was telling the truth. He could remember nothing of his departure in the outrigger, the way he had fought Shann in the lagoon. The Survey officer must have been under the control of the Warlockians then. Quickly he gave the older man his version of the other's actions in the outer world and Thorvald was clearly astounded, though he did not question the facts Shann presented.

"They just *took* me!" Thorvald said in a husky half whisper. "But why? And why are we here? Is this a prison?"

Shann shook his head. "I think all this"—a wave of his hand encompassed the green wall, what lay beyond it, and in it—"is a test of some kind. This dream business . . . A little while ago I got to thinking that I wasn't here at all, that I might be dreaming it all. Then I met you."

Thorvald understood. "Yes, but this *could* be a dream meeting. How can we tell?" He hesitated, almost diffidently, before he asked: "Have you met anyone else here?"

"Yes." Shann had no desire to go into that.

"People out of your past life?"

"Yes." Again he did not elaborate.

"So did I." Thorvald's expression was bleak; his encounters in the fog must have proved no more pleasant

142

than Shann's. "That suggests that we do trigger the hallucinations ourselves. But maybe we can really lick it now."

"How?"

"Well, if these phantoms are born of our memories there are about only two or three we could see together— maybe a Throg on the rampage, or that hound we left back in the mountains. And if we do sight anything like that, we'll know what it is. On the other hand, if we stick together and one of us sees something that the other can't . . . well, that fact alone will explode the ghost."

There was sense in what he said. Shann aided the officer to his feet.

"I must be a better subject for their experiments than you," the older man remarked ruefully. "They took me over completely at the first."

"You were carrying that disk," Shann pointed out. "Maybe that acted as a focusing lens for whatever power they use to make us play trained animals."

"Could be!" Thorvald brought out the cloth-wrapped bone coin. "I still have it." But he made no move to pull off the bit of rag about it. "Now"—he gazed at the wall of green—"which way?"

Shann shrugged. Long ago he had lost any idea of keeping a straight course through the murk. He might have turned around any number of times since he first walked blindly into this place. Then he pointed to the packet Thorvald held.

"Why not flip that?" he asked. "Heads, we go that way—" he indicated the direction in which they were facing—"tails, we do a rightabout-face."

There was an answering grin on Thorvald's lips. "As good a guide as any we're likely to find here. We'll do it." He pulled away the twist of cloth and with a swift snap, reminiscent of that used by the Warlockian witch to empty the bowl of sticks, he tossed the disk into the air.

It spun, whirled, but—to their open-jawed amazement —it did not fall to the sand. Instead it spun until it looked like a small globe instead of a disk. And it lost its dead white for a glow of green. When that glow became dazzling for Terran eyes the miniature sun swung out, not in orbit but in straight line of flight, heading to their right.

With a muffled cry, Thorvald started in pursuit, Shann running beside him. They were in a tunnel of the fog now, and the pace set by the spinning coin was swift. The Terrans continued to follow it at the best pace they could summon, having no idea of where they were headed, but each with the hope that they finally did have a guide to lead them through this place of confusion and into a sane world where they could face on more equal terms those who had sent them there.

14. ESCAPE

"SOMETHING ahead!" Thorvald did not slacken the pace set by the brilliant spot of green they trailed. Both of the Terrans feared to fall behind, to lose touch with that guide. Their belief that somehow the traveling disk would bring them to the end of the mist and its attendant illusions had grown firmer with every foot of ground they traversed.

A dark, fixed point, now partly veiled by mist, lay beyond, and it was toward that looming half-shadow that the spinning disk hurtled. Now the mist curled away to display its bulk—larger, blacker and four or five times Thorvald's height. Both men stopped short, for the disk no longer played path-finder. It still whirled on its axis in the air, faster and faster, until it appeared to be throwing off sparks, but the sparks faded against a monolith of dark rock unlike the native stone they had seen elsewhere. For it was neither red nor warmly brown, but a dull, dead black. It could have been a huge stone slab, trimmed, smoothed, set up on end as a monument or marker, except that only infinite labor could have accomplished such a task, and there was no valid reason for such toil as far as the Terrans could perceive.

"This is it." Thorvald moved closer.

By the disk's action, they deduced that their guide had drawn them to this featureless black steel with the precision of a beam-controlled ship. However, the purpose still eluded them. They had hoped for some exit from the territory of the veil, but now they faced a solid slab of dark stone, neither a conventional exit or entrance, as they proved by circling its base. Beneath their boots was the eternal sand, around them the fog.

"Now what?" Shann asked. They had made their trip about the slab and were back again where the disk whirled with unceasing vigor in a shower of emerald sparks.

Thorvald shook his head, scanning the rock face before them glumly. The eagerness had gone out of his expression, a vast weariness replacing it.

"There must have been some purpose in coming here," he replied, but his tone had lost the assurance of moments earlier.

"Well, if we strike away from here, we'll just get right back in again." Shann waved a hand toward the mist, waiting as if with a hunter's watch upon them. "And we certainly can't go down." He dug a boot toe into the sand to demonstrate the folly of that. "So, what about up?"

He ducked under the spinning disk to lay his hands against the surface of the giant slab. And in so doing he made a discovery, revealed to his touch although hidden from sight. For his fingers, running aimlessly across the cold, slightly uneven surface of the stone, slipped into a hollow, quite a deep hollow.

Excited, half fearing that his sudden guess might be wrong, Shann slid his hand higher in line with that hollow, to discover a second. The first had been level with his chest, the second perhaps eighteen inches or so above. He jumped, to draw his fingers down the rock, with damage to his nails but getting his proof. There *was* a third niche, deep enough to hold more than just the toe of a boot, and a fourth above that . . .

"We've a ladder of sorts here," he reported. Without waiting for any answer from Thorvald, Shann began to climb. The holds were so well matched in shape and size that he was sure they could not be natural; they had been bored there for use—the use to which he was now putting them—a ladder to the top of the slab. Though what he might find there was beyond his power to imagine.

The disk did not rise. Shann passed that core of light, climbing above it into the greater gloom. But the holes did not fail him; each was waiting in a direct line with its companion. And to an active man the scramble was not difficult. He reached the summit, glanced around, and made a quick grab for a secure handhold.

Waiting for him was no level platform such as he had confidently expected to find. The surface up which he had just made his way fly-fashion was the outer wall of a well or chimney. He looked down now into a pit where black nothingness began within a yard of the top, for the radiance of the mist did not penetrate far into that descent.

Shann fought an attack of giddiness. It would be very easy to lose control, to tumble over and be swallowed up in what might well be a bottomless chasm. And what was the purpose of this well? Was it a trap to entice a prisoner into an unwary climb and then let gravity drag him over? The whole setup was meaningless. Perhaps meaningless only to him, Shann conceded, with a flash of level thinking. The situation could be quite different as far as the natives were concerned. This structure did have a reason, or it would never have been erected in the first place.

"What's the matter?" Thorvald's voice was rough with impatience.

"This thing's a well." Shann edged about a fraction to call back. "The inside is open and—as far as I can tell—goes clear to the planet's core."

"Ladder on the inside too?"

Shann squirmed. That was, of course, a very obvious supposition. He kept a tight hold with his left hand, and with the other, he did some exploring. Yes, here was a hollow right enough, twin to those on the outside. But to swing over that narrow edge of safety and begin a descent into the black of the well was far harder than any action he had taken since the morning the Throgs had raided the camp. The green mist could hold no terrors greater than those with which his imagination peopled the depths now waiting to engulf him. But Shann swung over, fitted his boot into the first hollow, and started down.

The only encouragement he gained during that nightmare ordeal was that those holes were regularly spaced. But somehow his confidence did not feed on that fact. There always remained the nagging fear that when he searched for the next it would not be there and he would cling to his perch lacking the needful strength in aching arms and legs to reclimb the inside ladder.

He was fast losing that sense of well being which had been his during his travels through the fog; a fatigue tugged at his arms and weighed leaden on his shoulders. Mechanically he prospected for the next hold, and then the next. Above, the oblong of half-light grew smaller and smaller, sometimes half blotted out by the movements of Thorvald's body as the other followed him down that interior way.

How far *was* down? Shann giggled lightheadedly at the humor of that, or what seemed to be humor at the moment. He was certain that they were now below the level of the sand floor outside the slab. And yet no end had come to the well hollow.

No break of light down here; he might have been sightless. But just as the blind develop an extra perceptive sense of unseen obstacles, so did Shann now find that he was aware of a change in the nature of the space about him. His weary arms and legs held him against the solidity of a wall, yet the impression that there was no longer another wall at his back grew stronger with every niche which swung him downward. And he was as sure as if he could see it, that he was now in a wide-open space, another cavern, perhaps, but this one totally dark.

Deprived of sight, he relied upon his ears. And there was a sound, faint, distorted perhaps by the acoustics of this place, but keeping up a continuous murmur. Water! Not the wash of waves with their persistent beat, but rather the rippling of a running stream. Water must lie below!

And just as his weariness had grown with his leaving behind the fog, so now did both hunger and thirst gnaw at Shann, all the sharper for the delay. The Terran wanted to reach that water, could picture it in his mind, putting away the possibility—the probability—that it might be sea-born and salt, and so unfit to drink.

The upper opening to the cavern of the fog was now so far above him that he had to strain to see it. And that warmth which had been there was gone. A dank chill wrapped him here, dampened the holds to which he clung until he was afraid of slipping. While the murmur of the water grew louder, until its *slap-slap* sounded within arms' distance. His boot toe skidded from a niche. Shann fought to hold on with numbed fingers. The other foot went. He swung by his hands, kicking vainly to regain a measure of footing.

Then his arms could no longer support him, and he cried out as he fell. Water closed about him with an icy shock which for a moment paralyzed him. He flailed out, fighting the flood to get his head above the surface where he could gasp in precious gulps of air.

There was a current here, a swiftly running one. Shann remembered the one which had carried him into that cavern in which the Warlockians had their strange dwelling. Although there were no clusters of crystals in this tunnel to supply him with light, the Terran began to nourish a faint hope that he was again in that same stream, that those light crystals would appear, and that he might eventually return to the starting point of this meaningless journey.

So he strove only to keep his head above water. Hearing a splashing behind him, he called out: "Thorvald?"

"Lantee?" The answer came back at once; the splashing grew louder as the other swam to catch up.

Shann swallowed a mouthful of the water lapping against his chin. The taste was brackish, but not entirely salt, and though it stung his lips, the liquid relieved a measure of his thirst.

Only no glowing crystals appeared to stud these walls, and Shann's hope that they were on their way to the cavern of the island faded. The current grew swifter, and he had to fight to keep his head above water, his tired body reacting sluggishly to commands.

The murmur of the racing flood drummed louder in his ears, or was that sound the same? He could no longer be sure. Shann only knew that it was close to impossible to snatch the necessary breath as he was rolled over and over in the hurrying flood.

In the end he was ejected into blazing, blinding light, into a suffocation of wild water as the bullet in an ancient Terran rifle might have been fired at no specific target. Gasping, beaten, more than half-drowned, Shann was pummeled by waves, literally driven up on a rocky surface which skinned his body cruelly. He lay there, his arms moving feebly until he contrived to raise himself in time to be wretchedly sick. Somehow he crawled on a few feet farther before he subsided again, blinded by the light, flinching from the heat of the rocks on which he lay, but unable to do more for himself.

His first coherent thought was that his speculation concerning the reality of this experience was at last resolved. This could not possibly be an hallucination; at least this particular sequence of events was not. And he was still hazily considering that when a hand fell on his shoulder, fingers biting into his raw flesh.

Shann snarled, rolled over on his side. Thorvald, water dripping from his rags—or rather steaming from them— his shaggy hair plastered to his skull, sat there.

"You all right?"

Shan sat up in turn, shielding his smarting eyes. He was bruised, battered badly enough, but he could claim no major injuries.

"I think so. Where are we?"

Thorvald's lips stretched across his teeth in what was more a grimace than a smile. "Right off the map, any map I know. Take a look."

They were on a scrap of beach—beach which was more like a reef, for it lacked any covering comparable to sand except for some cupfuls of coarse gravel locked in rock depressions. Rocks, red as the rust of dried blood, rose in fantastic water-sculptured shapes around the small semi-level space they had somehow won.

This space was V-shaped, washed by equal streams on either side of the prong of rock by water which spouted from the face of a sheer cliff not too far away, with force enough to spray several feet beyond its exit point. Shann seeing that and guessing at its significance, drew a deep breath, and heard the ghost of an answering chuckle from his companion.

"Yes, that's where we came out, boy. Like to make a return trip?"

Shann shook his head, and then wished that he had not so rashly made that move, for the world swung in a dizzy whirl. Things had happened too fast. For the moment it was enough that they were out of the underground ways, back under the amber sky, feeling the bite of Warlock's sun.

Steadying his head with both hands, Shann turned slowly, to survey what might lie at their backs. The water, pouring by on either side, suggested that they were again on an island. Warlock, he thought gloomily, seemed to be for Terrans a succession of islands, all hard to escape.

The tangle of rocks did not encourage any exploration. Just gazing at them added to his weariness. They rose tier by tier, to a ragged crown against the sky. Shann continued to sit staring at them,

"To climb that . . ." His voice trailed into the silence of complete discouragement.

"You climb—or swim," Thorvald stated. But, Shann noted, the Survey officer was not in a hurry to make either move.

Nowhere in that wilderness of rock was there the least relieving bit of purple foliage. Nor did any clak-claks or leather-headed birds tour the sky over their heads. Shann's thirst might have been partially assuaged, but his hunger remained. And it was that need which forced him at last into action. The barren heights promised nothing in the way of food, but remembering the harvest the wolverines had taken from under the rocks along the river, he got to his feet and lurched out on the reef which had been their salvation, hunting some pool which might hold an edible captive or two.

So it was that Shann made the discovery of a possible path consisting of a ledge running toward the other end of the island, if this were an island where they had taken refuge. The spray of the water drenched that way, feeding small pools in the uneven surface, and strips of yellow weed trailed in slimy ribbons back below the surface of the waves.

He called to Thorvald and gestured to his find. And then, close together, linking hands when the going became hazardous, the men followed the path. Twice they made finds in the pools, finned or clawed grotesque creatures, which they killed and ate, wolfing down the few fragments of odd-tasting flesh. Then, in a small crevice, which could hardly be dignified by the designation of "cave," Thorvald chanced upon a quite exciting discovery —a clutch of four greenish eggs, each as large as his doubled fist.

Their outer covering was more like tough membrane than true shell, and the Terrans worried it open with difficulty. Shann shut his eyes, trying not to think of what he mouthed as he sucked his share dry. At least that semi-liquid stayed put in his middle, though he expected dis-astrous results from the experiment.

More than a little heartened by this piece of luck, they kept on, though the ledge changed from a reasonably level surface to a series of rising, unequal steps, drawing them away from the water. At long last they came to the end of that path. Shann leaned back against a convenient spur of rock.

"Company!" he alerted Thorvald.

The Survey officer joined him to share an outcrop of rock from which they were provided with an excellent view of the scene below, and it was a scene to hold their full attention.

That soft sweep of sand which had floored the cavern of the fog lay here also, a gray-blue carpet sloping gently out of the sea. For Shann had no doubt that the wide stretch of water before them was the western ocean. Walling the beach on either side, and extending well out into the water so that the farthest piles were awash ex-cept for their crowns, were pillars of stone, shaped with the same finish as that slab which had provided them a ladder of escape. And because of the regularity of their spacing, Shann did not believe them works of nature.

Grouped between them now were the players of the drama. One of the Warlockian witches, her gem body patterns glittering in the sunlight, was walking backward out of the sea, her hands held palms together, breast high, in a Terran attitude of prayer. And following her something swam in the water, clearly not another of her own species. But her actions suggested that by some in-visible means she was drawing that water dweller after her. Waiting on shore were two others of her kind, viewing her actions with close attention, the attention of scholars for an instructor.

"Wyverns!"

Shann looked inquiringly at his companion. Thorvald added a whisper of explanation. "A legend of Terra— they were supposed to have a snake's tail instead of hind legs, but the heads . . . They're Wyverns!"

Wyverns. Shann liked the sound of that word; to his mind it well fitted the Warlockian witches. And the one they were watching in action continued her steady backward retreat, rolling her bemused captive out of the water. What emerged into the blaze of sunlight was one of those fork-tailed sea dwellers such as the Terrans had seen die after the storm. The thing crawled out of the shallows, its eyes focused in a blind stare on the praying hands of the Wyvern.

She halted, well up on the sand, when the body of her victim or prisoner—Shann was certain that the fork-tail was one or the other—was completely out of the water. Then, with lightning speed, she dropped her hands.

Instantly fork-tail came to life. Fanged jaws snapped. Aroused, the beast was the incarnation of evil rage, a rage which had a measure of intelligence to direct it into deadly action. And facing it, seemingly unarmed and defenseless, were the slender, fragile Wyverns.

Yet none of the small group of natives made any attempt to escape. Shann thought them suicidal in their indifference as fork-tail, short legs sending the fine sand flying in a dust cloud, made a rush toward its enemies.

The Wyvern who had led the beast ashore did not move. But one of her companions swung up a hand, as if negligently waving the monster to a stop. Between her first two digits was a disk. Thorvald caught at Shann's arm.

"See that! It's a copy of the one I had; it must be!"

They were too far away to be sure it was a duplicate, but it was coin-shaped and bone-white. And now the Wyvern swung it back and forth in a metronome sweep. Fork-tail skidded to a stop, its head beginning—reluctantly at first, and then, with increasing speed—to echo that left-right sweep. This Wyvern had the sea beast under control, even as her companion had earlier held it.

Chance dictated what happened next. As had her sister charmer, the Wyvern began a backward withdrawal up the length of the beach, drawing the sea thing in her wake. They were very close to the foot of the drop above which the Terrans stood, fascinated, when the sand betrayed the witch. Her foot slipped into a hole and she was thrown backward, her control disk spinning out of her fingers.

At once the monster she had charmed shot forth its head, snapped at that spinning trifle—and swallowed it. Then the fork-tail hunched in a posture Shann had seen the wolverines use when they were about to spring. The weaponless Wyvern was the prey, and both her companions were too far away to interfere.

Why he moved he could not have explained. There was no reason for him to go to the aid of the Warlockian, one of the same breed who had ruled him against his will. But Shann sprang, landing in the sand on his hands and knees.

The sea thing whipped around, undecided between two possible victims. Shann had his knife free, was on his feet, his eyes on the beast's, knowing that he had appointed himself dragon slayer for no good reason.

15. DRAGON SLAYER

"Ayeeee!" Sheer defiance, not only of the beast he fronted, but of the Wyverns as well, brought that old rallying cry to his lips—the call used on the Dumps of Tyr to summon gang aid against outsiders. Fork-tail had crouched again for a spring, but that throat-crackling blast appeared to startle it.

Shann, blade ready, took a dancing step to the right. The thing was scaled, perhaps as well armored against frontal attack as was the shell-creature he had fought with the aid of the wolverines. He wished he had the Terran animals now—with Taggi and his mate to tease and feint about the monster, as they had done with the Throg hound—for he would have a better chance. If only the animals were here!

Those eyes—red-pitted eyes in a gargoyle head following his every movement—perhaps those were the only vulnerable points.

Muscles tensed beneath that scaled hide. The Terran readied himself for a sidewise leap, his knife hand raised to rake at those eyes. A brown shape with a V of lighter fur banding its back crossed the far range of Shann's vision. He could not believe what he saw, not even when a snarling animal, slavering with rage, came at a lumbering gallop to stand beside him, a second animal on its heels.

Uttering his own battle cry, Taggi attacked. The fork-tail's head swung, imitating the movements of the wolverine as it had earlier mimicked the swaying of the disk in the Wyvern's hand. Togi came in from the other side. They might have been hounds keeping a bull in play. And never had they shown such perfect team work, almost as if they could sense what Shann desired of them.

That forked tail lashed viciously, a formidable weapon. Bone, muscles, scaled flesh, half buried in the sand, swept up a cloud of grit into the face of the man and the animals. Shann fell back, pawing with his free hand at his eyes. The wolverines circled warily, trying for the attack they favored—the spring to the shoulders, the usually fatal assault on the spine behind the neck. But the armored head of the fork-tail, slung low, warned them off. Again the tail lashed, and this time Taggi was caught and hurled across the beach.

Togi uttered a challenge, made a reckless dash, and raked down the length of the fork-tail's body, fastening on that tail, weighing it to earth with her own poundage while the sea creature fought to dislodge her. Shann, his eyes watering from the sand, but able to see, watched that battle for a long second, judging that fork-tail was completely engaged in trying to free its best weapon from the grip of the wolverine. The latter clawed and bit with a fury which suggested Togi intended to immobilize that weapon by tearing it to shreds.

Fork-tail wrenched its body, striving to reach its tormentor with fangs or clawed feet. And in that struggle to achieve an impossible position, its head slued far about, uncovering the unprotected area behind the skull base which usually lay under the spiny collar about its shoulders.

Shann went in. With one hand he gripped the edge of that collar—its serrations tearing his flesh—and at the

same time he drove his knife blade deep into the sof
underfolds, ripping on toward the spinal column. The
blade nicked against bone as the fork-tail's head slammed
back, catching Shann's hand and knife together in a trap
The Terran was jerked from his feet, and flung to one
side with the force of the beast's reaction.

Blood spurted up, his own blood mingled with that o
the monster. Only Togi's riding of the tail prevented
Shann's being beaten to death. The armored snou
pointed skyward as the creature ground the sharp edge
of its collar down on the Terran's arm. Shann, frantic
with pain, drove his free fist into one of those eyes.

Fork-tail jerked convulsively; its head snapped down
again and Shann was free. The Terran threw himsel
back, keeping his feet with an effort. Fork-tail wa
writhing, churning up the sand in a cloud. But it could
not rid itself of the knife Shann had planted with all his
strength, and which the blows of its own armored collar
were now driving deeper and deeper into its back.

It howled thinly, with an abnormal shrilling. Shann
nursing his bleeding forearm against his chest, rolled free
from the waves of sand it threw about, bringing up
against one of the rock pillars. With that to steady him
he somehow found his feet, and stood weaving, trying to
see through the rain of dust.

The convulsions which churned up that concealing
cloud were growing more feeble. Then Shann heard the
triumphant squall from Togi, saw her brown body still on
the torn tail just above the forking. The wolverine used
her claws to hitch her way up the spine of the sea monster, heading for the mountain of blood spouting from
behind the head. Fork-tail fought to raise that head once
more; then the massive jaw thudded into the sand, teeth
snapping fruitlessly as a flood of grit overrode the tongue,
packed into the gaping mouth.

How long had it taken—that frenzy of battle on the bloodstained beach? Shann could have set no limit in clock-ruled time. He pressed his wounded arm tighter to him, lurched past the still twitching sea thing to that splotch of brown fur on the sand, shaping the wolverine's whistle with dry lips. Togi was still busy with the kill, but Taggi lay where that murderous tail had thrown him.

Shann fell on his knees, as the beach around him developed a curious tendency to sway. He put his good hand to the ruffled back fur of the motionless wolverine.

"Taggi!"

A slight quiver answered. Shann tried awkwardly to raise the animal's head with his own hand. As far as he could see, there were no open wounds; but there might be broken bones, internal injuries he did not have the skill to heal.

"Taggi?" He called again gently, striving to bring that heavy head up on his knee.

"The furred one is not dead."

For a moment Shann was not aware that those words had formed in his mind, had not been heard by his ears. He looked up, eyes blazing at the Wyvern coming toward him in a graceful glide across the crimsoned sand. And in a space of heartbeats his thrust of anger cooled into a stubborn enmity.

"No thanks to you," he said deliberately aloud. If the Wyvern witch wanted to understand him, let her make the effort; he did not try to touch her thoughts with his.

Taggi stirred again, and Shann glanced down quickly. The wolverine gasped, opened his eyes, shook his miniature bear head, scattering pellets of sand. He sniffed at a dollop of blood, the dark, alien blood, spattered on Shann's breeches, and then his head came up with a reassuring alertness as he looked to where his mate was still worrying the now quiet fork-tail.

With an effort, Taggi got to his feet, Shann aiding him. The man ran his hand down over ribs, seeking any broken bones. Taggi growled a warning once when that examination brought pain in its wake, but Shann could detect no real damage. As might a cat, the wolverine must have met the shock of that whip-tail stroke relaxed enough to escape serious injury. Taggi had been knocked out, but now he was able to navigate again. He pulled free from Shann's grip, lumbering across the sand to the kill.

Someone else was crossing that strip of beach. Passing the Wyvern as if he did not see them, Thorvald came directly to Shann. A few seconds later he had the torn arm stretched across his own bent knee, examining the still bleeding hurt.

"That's a nasty one," he commented.

Shann heard the words and they made sense, but the instability of his surroundings was increasing, while Thorvald's handling sent sharp stabs of pain up his arm and somehow into his head, where they ended in red bursts to cloud his sight.

Out of the reddish mist which had fogged most of the landscape there emerged a single object, a round white disk. And in Shann's clouded mind a well-rooted apprehension stirred. He struck out with his one hand, and through luck connected. The disk flew out of sight. His vision cleared enough so he could sight the Wyvern who had been leaning over Thorvald's shoulder centering her weird weapon on him. Making a great effort, Shann got out the words, words which he also shaped in his mind as he said them aloud: "You're not taking me over—again!"

There was no emotion to be read on that jewel-banded

face or in her unblinking eyes. He caught at Thorvald, determined to get across his warning.

"Don't let them use those disks on us!"

"I'll do my best."

Only the haze had taken Thorvald again. Did one of the Wyverns have a disk focused on them? Were they being pulled into one of those blank periods, to awaken as prisoners once more—say, in the cavern of the veil? The Terran fought with every ounce of will power to escape unconsciousness, but he failed.

This time he did not awaken half-drowning in an underground stream or facing a green mist. And there was an ache in his arm which was somehow reassuring with the very insistence of pain. Before opening his eyes, his fingers crossed the smooth slick of a bandage there, went on to investigate by touch a sleep mat such as he had found in the cavern structure. Was he back in that web of rooms and corridors?

Shann delayed opening his eyes until a kind of shame drove him to it. He first saw an oval opening almost the length of his body as it was stretched only a foot or two below the sill of that window. And through its transparent surface came the golden light of the sun—no green mist, no crystals mocking the stars.

The room in which he lay was small with smooth walls, much like that in which he had been imprisoned on the island. And there were no other furnishings save the mat on which he rested. Over him was a light cover netted of fibers resembling yarn, with feathers knotted into it to provide a downy upper surface. His clothing was gone, but the single covering was too warm and he pushed it away from his shoulders and chest as he wriggled up to see the view beyond the window.

His torn arm came into full view. From wrist to elbow it was encased in an opaque skin sheath, unlike any bandage of his own world. Surely that had not come out of any Survey aid pack. Shann gazed toward the window but beyond lay only a reach of sky. Except for a lemon cloud or two ruffled high above the horizon, nothing broke that soft amber curtain. He might be quartered in a tower well above ground level, which did not match his former experience with Wyvern accommodations.

"Back with us again?" Thorvald, one hand lifting a door panel, came in. His ragged uniform was gone, and he wore only breeches of a sleek green material and his own scuffed-and-battered boots.

Shann settled back on the mat. "Where are we?"

"I think you might term this the capital city," Thorvald answered. "In relation to the mainland, we're on an island well out to sea—westward."

"How did we get here?" That climb in the slab, the stream underground . . . Had it been an interior river running under the bed of the sea? But Shann was not prepared for the other's reply.

"By wishing."

"By *what?*"

Thorvald nodded, his expression serious. "They wished us here. Listen, Lantee, when you jumped down to mix it with that fork-tailed thing, did you wish you had the wolverines with you?"

Shann thought back; his memories of what had occured before that battle were none too clear. But, yes, he had wished Taggi and Togi present at that moment to distract the enraged beast.

"You mean I wished them?" The whole idea was probably a part of the Wyvern jargon of dreaming and he added, "Or did I just dream everything?" There was the bandage on his arm, the soreness under that bandage. But also there had been Logally's lash brand back in the cavern, which had bitten into his flesh with the pain of a real blow.

"No, you weren't dreaming. You happened to be tuned in on one of those handy little gadgets our lady friends here use. And, so tuned in, your desire for the wolverines being pretty powerful just then, they came."

Shann grimaced. This was unbelievable. Yet there were his meetings with Logally and Trav. How could anyone rationally explain them? And how had he, in the beginning, been jumped from the top of the cliff on the island of his marooning into the midst of an underground flood without any conscious memory of an intermediate journey?

"How does it work?" he asked simply.

Thorvald laughed. "You tell me. They have these disks, one to a Wyvern, and they control forces with them. Back there on the beach we interrupted a class in such control; they were the novices learning their trade. We've tumbled on something here which can't be defined or understood by any of our previous standards of comparison. It's frankly magic, judged by our terms."

"Are we prisoners?" Shann wanted to know.

"Ask me something I'm sure of. I've been free to come and go within limits. No one's exhibited any signs of hostility; most of them simply ignore me. I've had two interviews, via this mind-reading act of theirs, with their rulers, or elders, or chief sorceresses—all three titles seem to apply. They ask questions, I answer as best I can, but sometimes we appear to have no common meeting ground. Then I ask some questions, they evade gracefully, or reply in a kind of unintelligible double-talk, and that's as far as our communication has progressed so far."

"Taggi and Togi?"

"Have a run of their own and as far as I can tell are

better satisfied with life than I am. Oddly enough, they respond more quickly and more intelligently to orders Perhaps this business of being shunted around by th disks has conditioned them in some way."

"What about these Wyverns? Are they all female?"

"No, but their tribal system is strictly matriarcha which follows a pattern even Terra once knew: the fertil earth mother and her priestesses, who became th witches when the gods overruled the goddesses. Th males are few in number and lack the power to activat the disks. In fact," Thorvald laughed ruefully, "one gath ers that in this civilization our opposite numbers have more or less, the status of pets at the best, and necessar evils at the worst. Which put *us* at a disadvantage from the start."

"You think that they won't take us seriously because w are males?"

"Might just work out that way. I've tried to ge through to them about danger from the Throgs, tellin them what it would mean to them to have the beetle heads settle in here for good. They just brush aside th whole idea."

"Can't you argue that the Throgs are males, too? O aren't they?"

The Survey officer shook his head. "That's a point n human can answer. We've been sparring with Throgs fo years and there have been libraries of reports writte about them and their behavior patterns, all of which ad up to about two paragraphs of proven facts and hun dreds of surmises beginning with the probable anc skimming out into the wild fantastic. You can claim any thing about a Throg and find a lot of very intelligen souls ready to believe you. But whether those beetle heads squatting over on the mainland are able to answe to 'he,' 'she,' or 'it,' your solution is just as good as mine.

We've always considered the ones we fight to be males, but they might just as possibly be amazons. Frankly, these Wyverns couldn't care less either; at least that's the impression they give."

"But anyway," Shann observed, "it hasn't come to 'we're all girls together' either."

Thorvald laughed again. "Not so you can notice. We're not the only unwilling visitor in the vicinity."

Shann sat up. "A Throg?"

"A something. Non-Warlockian, or non-Wyvern. And perhaps trouble for us."

"You haven't seen this other?"

Thorvald sat down cross-legged. The amber light from the window made red-gold of his hair, added ruddiness to his less-gaunt features.

"No, I haven't. As far as I can tell, the stranger's not right here. I caught stray thought beams twice—surprise expressed by newly arrived Wyverns who met me and apparently expected to be fronted by something quite physically different."

"Another Terran scout?"

"No. I imagine that to the Wyverns we must look a lot alike. Just as we couldn't tell one of them from her sister if their body patterns didn't differ. Discovered one thing about those patterns—the more intricate they run, the higher the 'power,' not of the immediate wearer, but of her ancestors. They're marked when they qualify for their disk and presented with the rating of the greatest witch in their family line as an inducement to live up to those deeds and surpass them if possible. Quite a bit of logic to that. Given the right conditioning, such a system might even work in our service.

That nugget of information was the stuff from which Survey reports were made. But at the moment the information concerning the other captive was of more value to

Shann. He steadied his body against the wall with his good hand and got to his feet. Thorvald watched him.

"I take it you have visions of action. Tell me, Lantee, why *did* you take that header off the cliff to mix it with fork-tail?"

Shann wondered himself. He had no reason for that impulsive act. "I don't know—"

"Chivalry? Fair Wyvern in distress?" the other prodded. "Or did the back lash from one of those disks draw you in?"

"I don't know—"

"And why did you use your knife instead of your stunner?"

Shann was startled. For the first time he realized that he had fronted the greatest native menace they had discovered on Warlock with the more primitive of his weapons. Why had he not tried the stunner on the beast? He had just never thought of it when he had taken that leap into the role of dragon slayer.

"Not that it would have done you any good to try the ray; it has no effect on fork-tail."

"You tried it?"

"Naturally. But you didn't know that, or did you pick up that information earlier?"

"No," answer Shann slowly. "No, I don't know why I used the knife. The stunner would have been more natural." Suddenly he shivered, and. the face he turned to Thorvald was very sober.

"How much do they control us?" he asked, his voice dropping to a half whisper as if the walls about them could pick up those words and relay them to other ears. "What can they do?"

"A good qiestion." Thorvald lost his light tone. "Yes, what can they feed into our minds without our knowing? Perhaps those disks are only window dressing, and they can work without them. A great deal will depend upon the impression we can make on these witches." He began to smile again, more wryly. "The name we gave this planet is certainly a misnomer. A warlock is a male sorcerer, not a witch."

"And what are the chances of our becoming warlocks ourselves?"

Again Thorvald's smile faded, but he gave a curt little nod to Shann as if approving that thought. "That is something we are going to look into, and now! If we have to convince some stubborn females, as well as fight Throgs, well"—he shrugged—"we'll have a busy, busy, time."

16. THIRD PRISONER

"WELL, it works as good as new." Shann held his hand and arm out into the full path of the sun. He had just stripped off the skin-case bandage, to show the raw seam of a half-healed scar, but as he flexed muscles, bent and twisted his arm, there was only a small residue of soreness left.

"Now what, or where?" he asked Thorvald with some eagerness. Several days' imprisonment in this room had made him impatient for the outer world again. Like the officer, he now wore breeches of the green fabric, the only material known to the Wyverns, and his own badly worn boots. Oddly enough, the Terrans' weapons, stunner and knife, had been left to them, a point which made them uneasy, since it suggested that the Wyverns believed they had nothing to fear from clumsy alien arms.

"Your guess is as good as mine," Thorvald answered

that double question. "But it is you they want to see; they insisted upon it, rather emphatically in fact."

The Wyvern city existed as a series of cell-like hollows in the interior of a rock-walled island. Outside there had been no tampering with the natural rugged features of the escarpment, and within, the silence was almost complete. For all the Terrans could learn, the population of the stone-walled hive might have been several thousand, or just the handful that they had seen with their own eyes along the passages which had been declared open territory for them.

Shann half expected to find again a skull-walled chamber where witches tossed colored sticks to determine his future. But he came with Thorvald into an oval room in which most of the outer wall was a window. And seeing what lay framed in that, Shann halted, again uncertain as to whether he actually saw that, or whether he was willed into visualizing a scene by the choice of his hostesses.

They were lower now than the room in which he had nursed his wound, not far above water level. And this window faced the sea. Across a stretch of green water was his red-purple skull, the waves lapping its lower jaw, spreading their foam in between the gaping rock-fringe which formed its teeth. And from the eye hollows flapped the clak-claks of the sea coast, coming and going as if they carried to some imprisoned brain within that giant bone case messages from the outer world.

"My dream—" Shann said.

"Your dream." Thorvald had not echoed that; the answer had come in his brain.

Shann turned his head and surveyed the Wyvern awaiting them with a concentration which was close to the rudeness of an outright stare, a stare which held no friendship. For by her skin patterns he knew her for the

ne who had led that triumvir who had sent him into the
cavern of the mist. And with her was the younger witch
he had trapped on the night that all this baffling action
had begun.

"We meet again," he said slowly. "To what purpose?"

"To our purpose . . . and yours—"

"I do not doubt that it is to yours." The Terran's
thoughts fell easily now into a formal pattern he would
not have used with one of his own kind. "But I do not
expect any good to me. . . ."

There was no readable expression on her face; he did
not expect to see any. But in their uneven mind touch he
caught a fleeting suggestion of bewilderment on her part,
as if she found his mental processes as hard to understand as a puzzle with few leading clues.

"We mean you no ill, star voyager. You are far more
than we first thought you, for you have dreamed false
and have known. Now dream true, and know it also."

"Yet," he challenged, "you would set me a task without
my consent."

"We have a task for you, but already it was set in the
pattern of your true dreaming. And we do not set such
patterns, star man; that is done by the Greatest Power of
all. Each lives within her appointed pattern from the
First Awakening to the Final Dream. So we do not ask of
you any more than that which is already laid for your
doing."

She arose with that languid grace which was a part of
their delicate jeweled bodies and came to stand beside
him, a child in size, making his Terran flesh and bones
awkward, clodlike in contrast. She stretched out her four-
digit hand, her slender arm ringed with gemmed circles
and bands, measuring it beside his own, bearing that
livid scar.

"We are different, star man, yet still are we both

dreamers. And dreams hold power. Your dreams brough⸗
you across the dark which lies between sun and distan⸗
sun. Our dreams carry us on even stranger roads. An⸗
yonder"—one of her fingers stiffened to a point, indicat⸗
ing the skull—"there is another who dreams with power
a power which will destroy us all unless the pattern i⸗
broken speedily."

"And I must go to seek this dreamer?" His vision o⸗
climbing through that nose hole was to be realized
then.

"You go."

Thorvald stirred and the Wyvern turned her head t⸗
him. "Alone," she added. "For this is your dream only, a⸗
it has been from the beginning. There is for each his ow⸗
dream, and another cannot walk through it to alter th⸗
pattern, even to save a life."

Shann grinned crookedly, without humor. "It seem⸗
that I'm elected," he said as much to himself as to Thor⸗
vald. "But what do I do with this other dreamer?"

"What your pattern moves you to do. Save that you d⸗
not slay him—"

"Throg!" Thorvald started forward. "You can't jus⸗
walk in on a Throg barehanded and be bound by orders
such as that!"

The Wyvern must have caught the sense of that vocal
protest, for her communication touched them both. "W⸗
cannot deal with that one as his mind is closed to us. Ye⸗
he is an elder among his kind and his people have been
searching land and sea for him since his air rider broke
upon the rocks and he entered into hiding over there.
Make your peace with him if you can, and also take hi⸗
hence, for his dreams are not ours, and he brings confusion to the Reachers when they retire to run the Trails of
Seeking."

"Must be an important Throg," Shann deduced. "They

could have an officer of the beetle-heads under wraps over there. Could we use him to bargain with the rest?"

Thorvald's frown did not lighten. "We've never been able to establish any form of contact in the past, though our best qualified minds, reinforced by training, have tried ..."

Shann did not take fire at that rather delicate estimate of his own lack of preparation for the carrying out of diplomatic negotiations with the enemy; he knew it was true. But there was one thing he could try—if the Wyverns permitted.

"Will you give a disk of power to this star man?" He pointed to Thorvald. "For he is my Elder One and a Reacher for Knowledge. With such a focus his dream could march with mine when I go to the Throg, and perhaps that can aid in my doing what I could not accomplish alone. For that is the secret of *my* people, Elder One. We link our powers together to make a shield against our enemies, a common tool for the work we must do."

"And so it is with us also, star voyager. We are not so unlike as the foolish might think. We learned much of you while you both wandered in the Place of False Dreams. But our power disks are our own and can not be given to a stranger while their owners live. However ..." She turned again with an abruptness foreign to the usual Wyvern manner and faced the older Terran.

The officer might have been obeying an unvoiced order as he put out his hands and laid them palm to palm on those she held up to him, bending his head so gray eyes met golden ones. The web of communication which had held all three of them snapped. Thorvald and the Wyvern were linked in a tight circuit which excluded Shann.

Then the latter became conscious of movement beside

him. The younger Wyvern had joined him to watch the clak-claks in their circling of the bare dome of the skull island.

"Why do they fly so?" Shann asked her.

"Within they nest, care for their young. Also they hunt the rock creatures that swarm in the lower darkness."

"The rock creatures?" If the skull's interior was infested by some other native fauna, he wanted to know it.

By some method of her own the young Wyvern conveyed a strong impression of revulsion, which was her personal reaction to the "rock creatures."

"Yet you imprison the Throg there—" he remarked.

"Not so!" Her denial was instantaneous and vehement. "The other worlder fled into that place in spite of our calling. There he stays in hiding. Once we drew him out to the sea, but he broke the power and fled inside again."

"Broke free—" Shann pounced upon that. "From disk control?"

"But surely." Her reply held something of wonder. "Why do you ask, star voyager? Did you not also break free from the power of the disk when I led you by the underground ways, awaking in the river? Do you then rate this other one as less than your own breed that you think him incapable of the same action?"

"Of Throgs I know as much as this . . ." He held up his hand, measuring off a fraction of space between thumb and forefinger.

"Yet you knew them before you came to this world."

"My people have known them for long. We have met and fought many times among the stars."

"And never have you talked mind to mind?"

"Never. We have sought for that, but there has been no communication between us, neither of mind nor of voice."

"This one you name Throg is truly not as you," she

172

assented. "And we are not as you, being alien and female. Yet, star man, you and I have shared a dream."

Shann stared at her, startled, not so much by what she said as the human shading of those words in his mind. Or had that also been illusion?

"In the veil . . . that creature which came to you on wings when you remembered that. A good dream, though it came out of the past and so was false in the present. But I have gathered it into my own store: such a fine dream, one that you have cherished."

"Trav was to be cherished," he agreed soberly. "I found her in a broken sleep cage at a spaceport when I was a child. We were both cold and hungry, alone and hurt. So I stole and was glad that I stole Trav. For a little space we both were very happy . . ." Forcibly he stifled memory.

"So, though we are unlike in body and in mind, yet we find beauty together if only in a dream. Therefore, between your people and mine there can *be* a common speech. And I may show you my dream store for your enjoyment, star voyager."

A flickering of pictures, some weird, some beautiful, all a little distorted—not only by haste, but also by the haze of alienness which was a part of her memory pattern—crossed Shann's mind.

"Such a sharing would be a rich feast," he agreed.

"All right!" Those crisp words in his own tongue brought Shann away from the window to Thorvald. The Survey officer was no longer locked hand to hand with the Wyvern witch, but his features were alive with a new eagerness.

"We are going to try your idea, Lantee. They'll provide me with a new, unmarked disk, show me how to use it. And I'll do what I can to back you with it. But they insist that you go today."

173

"What do they really want me to do? Just route out that Throg? Or try to talk him into being a go-between with his people? That *does* come under the heading of dreaming!"

"They want him out of there, back with his own kind if possible. Apparently he's a disruptive influence for them; he causes some kind of a mental foul up which interferes drastically with their 'power.' They haven't been able to get him to make any contact with them. This Elder One is firm about your being the one ordained for the job, and that you'll know what action to take when you get there."

"Must have thrown the sticks for me again," Shann commented.

"Well, they've definitely picked you to smoke out the Throg, and they can't be talked into changing their minds about that."

"I'll be the smoked one if he has a blaster."

"They say he's unarmed—"

"What do they know about our weapons or a Throg's?"

"The other one has no arms." Wyvern words in his mind again. "This fact gives him great fear. That which he has depended upon is broken. And since he has no weapon, he is shut into a prison of his own terrors."

But an adult Throg, even unarmed, was not to be considered easy meat, Shann thought. Armored with horny skin, armed with claws and those crushing mandibles of the beetle mouth . . . a third again as tall as he himself was. No, even unarmed, the Throg had to be considered a menace.

Shann was still thinking along that line as he splashed through the surf which broke about the lower jaw of the skull island, climbed up one of the pointed rocks which masqueraded as a tooth, and reached for a higher hold to lead him to the nose slit, the gateway to the alien's hiding place.

The clak-claks screamed and dived about him, highly resentful of his intrusion. And when they grew so bold as to buffet him with their wings, threaten him with their tearing beaks, he was glad to reach the broken rock edging his chosen door and duck inside. Once there, Shann looked back. There was no sighting the cliff window where Thorvald stood, nor was he aware in any way of mental contact with the Survey officer; their hope of such a linkage might be futile.

Shann was reluctant to venture farther. His eyes had sufficiently adjusted to the limited supply of light, and now the Terran brought out the one aid the Wyverns had granted him, a green crystal such as those which had played the roll of stars on the cavern roof. He clipped its simple loop setting to the front of his belt, leaving his hands free. Then, having filled his lungs for the last time with clean, sea-washed air, he started into the dome of the skull.

There was a fetid thickness to this air only a few feet away from the outer world. The odor of clak-clak droppings and refuse from their nests was strong, but there was an added staleness, as if no breeze ever scooped out the old atmosphere to replace it with new. Fragile bones crunched under Shann's boots, but as he drew away from the entrance, the pale glow of the crystal increased its radiance, emitting a light not unlike that of the phosphorescent bushes, so that he was not swallowed up by dark.

The cave behind the nose hole narrowed quickly into a cleft, a narrow cleft which pierced into the bowl of the skull. Shann proceeded with caution, pausing every few steps. There came a murmur rising now and again to a shriek, issuing, he guessed, from the clak-clak rookery above. And the pound of sea waves was also a vibration carrying through the rock. He was listening for something else, at the same time testing the ill-smelling air for that betraying muskiness which spelled Throg.

When a twist in the narrow passage cut off the splotch of daylight, Shann drew his stunner. The strongest bolt from that could not jolt a Throg into complete paralysis, but it would slow up any attack.

Red—pinpoints of red—were edging a break in the rock wall. They were gone in a flash. Eyes? Perhaps of the rock dwellers which the Wyverns hated? More red dots, farther ahead. Shann listened for a sound he could identify.

But smell came before sound. That trace of effluvia which in force could sicken a Terran, was his guide. The cleft ended in a space to which the limited gleam of the crystal could not provide a far wall. But that faint light did show him his quarry.

The Throg was not on his feet, ready for trouble, but hunched close to the wall. And the alien did not move at Shann's coming. Did the beetle-head sight him? Shann wondered. He moved cautiously. And the round head, with its bulbous eyes, turned a fraction; the mandibles about the ugly mouth opening quivered. Yes, the Throg could see him.

But still the alien made no move to rise out of his crouch, to come at the Terran. Then Shann saw the fall of rock, the stone which pinned a double-kneed leg to the floor. And in a circle about the prisoner were the small, crushed, furred things which had come to prey on the helpless to be slain themselves by the well-aimed stones which were the Throg's only weapons of defense.

Shann sheathed his stunner. It was plain the Throg was helpless and could not reach him. He tried to concentrate mentally on a picture of the scene before him, hoping that Thorvald or one of the Wyverns could pick it up.

There was no answer, no direction. Choice of action remained soley his.

The Terran made the oldest friendly gesture of his kind; his empty hands held up, palm out. There was no answering move from the Throg. Neither of the other's upper limbs stirred, their claws still gripping the small rocks in readiness for throwing. All Shann's knowledge of the alien's history argued against an unarmed advance. The Throg's marksmanship, as borne out by the circle of small bodies, was excellent. And one of those rocks might well thud against his own head, with fatal results. Yet he had been sent there to get the Throg free and out of Wyvern territory.

So rank was the beetle smell of the other that Shann coughed. What he needed now was the aid of the wolverines, a diversion to keep the alien busy. But this time there was no disk working to produce Taggi and Togi out of thin air. And he could not continue to just stand there staring at the Throg. There remained the stunner. Life on the Dumps tended to make a man a fast draw, a matter of survival for the fastest and most accurate marksman. And now one of Shann's hands swept down with a speed which, learned early, was never really to be forgotten.

He had the rod out and was spraying on tight beam straight at the Throg's head before the first stone struck his shoulder and his weapon fell from a numbed hand. But a second stone tumbled out of the Throg's claw. The alien tried to reach for it, his movements slow, uncertain.

Shann, his arm dangling, went in fast, bracing his good shoulder against the boulder which pinned the Throg. The alien aimed a blow at the Terran's head, but again so slowly Shann had no difficulty in evading it. The boulder gave, rolled, and Shanned cleared out of range, back to the opening of the cleft, pausing only to scoop up his stunner.

For a long moment the Throg made no move; his dazed wits must have been working at very slow speed. Then the alien heaved up his body to stand erect, favoring the leg which had been trapped. Shann tensed, waiting for a rush. What now? Would the Throg refuse to move? If so, what could he do about it?

With the impact of a blow, the message Shann had hoped for struck into his mind. But his initial joy at that contact was wiped out with the same speed.

"Throg ship . . . overhead."

The Throg stood away from the wall, limped out, heading for Shann, or perhaps only the cleft in which he stood. Swinging the stunner awkwardly in his left hand, the Terran retreated, mentally trying to contact Thorvald once more. There was no answer. He was well up into the cleft, moving crabwise, unwilling to turn his back on the Throg. The alien was coming as steadily as his injured limb would allow, trying for the exit to the outer world.

A Throg ship overhead . . . Had the castaway somehow managed to call his own kind? And what if he, Shann Lantee, were to be trapped between the alien and a landing party from the flyer? He did not expect any assistance from the Wyverns, and what could Thorvald possibly do? From behind him, at the entrance of the nose slit, he heard a sound—a sound which was neither the scolding of a clak-clak nor the eternal growl of the sea.

17. THROG JUSTICE

THE musty stench was so strong that Shann could no longer fight the demands of his outraged stomach. He rolled on his side, retching violently until the sour smell of his illness battled the foul odor of the ship. His memories of how he had come into this place were vague; his body was a mass of dull pain, as if he had been scorched. Scorched! Had the Throgs used one of their energy whips to subdue him? The last clear thing he could recall was that slow withdrawal down the cleft inside the skull rock, the Throg not too far away—the sound from the entrance.

A Throg prisoner! Through the pain and the sickness the horror of that bit doubly deep. Terrans did not fall alive into Throg hands, not if they had the means of ending their existence within reach. But his hands and arms were caught behind him in an unbreakable lock, some gadget not unlike the Terran force bar used to restrain criminals, he decided groggily.

The cubby in which he lay was black-dark. But the quivering of the deck and the bulkheads about him told Shann that the ship was in flight. And there could be but two destinations, either the camp where the Throg force had taken over the Terran installations or the mother ship of the raiders. If Thorvald's earlier surmise was true and the aliens were hunting a Terran to talk in the transport, then they were heading for the camp.

And because a man who still lives and who is not yet broken can also hope, Shann began to think ahead to the camp—the camp and a faint, thin chance of escape. For on the surface of Warlock there was a thin chance; in the mother ship of the Throgs none at all.

Thorvald—and the Wyverns! Could he hope for any help from them? Shann closed his eyes against the thick darkness and tried to reach out to touch, somewhere, Thorvald with his disk—or perhaps the Wyvern who had talked of Trav and shared dreams. Shann focused his thoughts on the young Wyvern witch, visualizing with all the detail he could summon out of memory the brilliant patterns about her slender arms, her thin, fragile wrists, those other designs overlaying her features. He could see her in his mind, but she was only a puppet, without life, certainly without power.

Thorvald . . . Now Shann fought to build a mental picture of the Survey officer, making his stand at that window, grasping his disk, with the sun bringing gold to his hair and showing the bronze of his skin. Those gray eyes which could be ice, that jaw with the tight set of a trap upon occasion . . .

And Shann made contact! He touched something, a flickering like a badly tuned tri-dee—far more fuzzy than the mind pictures the Wyvern had paraded for him. But he had touched! And Thorvald, too, had been aware of his contact.

Shann fought to find that thread of awareness again. Patiently he once more created his vision of Thorvald, adding every detail he could recall, small things about the other which he had not known that he had noticed— the tiny arrow-shaped scar near the base of the officer's throat, the way his growing hair curled at the ends, the look of one eyebrow slanting abruptly toward his hairline when he was dubious about something. Shann strove to make a figure as vividly as Logally and Trav had been in the mist of the illusion.

". . . where?"

This time Shann was prepared; he did not let that mind image dissolve in his excitement at recapturing the link. "Throg ship," he said the words aloud, over and over, but still he held to his picture of Thorvald.

". . . will . . ."

Only that one word! The thread between them snapped again. Only then did Shann become conscious of a change in the ship's vibration. Were they setting down? And where? Let it be at the camp! It must be the camp!

There was no jar at that landing, just that one second the vibration told him the ship was alive and air-borne, and the next a dead quiet testified that they had landed. Shann, his sore body stiff with tension, waited for the next move on the part of his captors.

He continued to lie in the dark, still queasy from the stench of the cell, too keyed up to try to reach Thorvald. There was a dull grating over his head, and he looked up eagerly—to be blinded by a strong beam of light. Claws hooked painfully under his arms and he was manhandled up and out, dragged along a short passage and pitched free of the ship, falling hard upon trodden earth and rolling over gasping as the seared skin of his body was rasped and abraded.

The Terran lay face up now, and as his eyes adjusted to the light, he saw a ring of Throg heads blotting out the sky as they inspected their catch impassively. The mouth mandibles of one moved with a faint clicking. Again claws fastened in his armpits, brought Shann to his feet, holding him erect.

Then the Throg who had given that order moved closer. His hand-claws clasped a small metal plate surmounted by a hoop of thin wire over which was stretched

a web of threads glistening in the sun. Holding that hoop
on a level with his mouth, the alien clicked his mandibles
and those sounds became barely distinguishable basic
galactic words.

"You Throg meat!".

For a moment Shann wondered if the alien meant that
statement literally. Or was it a conventional expression
for a prisoner among their kind.

"Do as told!"

That was clear enough, and for the moment the Terran
did not see that he had any choice in the matter. But
Shann refused to make any sign of agreement to either of
those two limited statements. Perhaps the beetle-head
did not expect any. The alien who had pulled him to his
feet continued to hold him erect, but the attention of the
Throg with the translator switched elsewhere.

From the alien ship emerged a second party. The
Throg in their midst was unarmed and limping. Although
to Terran eyes one alien was the exact counterpart of the
other, Shann thought that this one was the prisoner in the
skull cave. Yet the indications now suggested that he had
only changed one captivity for another and was in dis
grace among his kind. Why?

The Throg limped up to front the leader with the
translator, and his guards fell back. Again mandibles
clicked, were answered, though the sense of that ex
change eluded Shann. At one point in the report—if re
port it was—he himself appeared to be under discussion
for the injured Throg waved a hand-claw in the Terran's
direction. But the end to the conference came quickly
enough and in a manner which Shann found shock
ing.

Two of the guards stepped forward, caught at the in
jured Throg's arms and drew him away, leading him out
into a space beyond the grounded ship. They dropped

their hold on him, returning at a trot. The officer clicked an order. Blasters were unholstered, and the Throg in the field shriveled under a vicious concentration of cross bolts. Shann gasped. He certainly had no liking for Throgs, but this execution carried overtones of a cold-blooded ferocity which transcended anything he had known, even in the callous brutality of the Dumps.

Limp, and more than a little sick again, he watched the Throg officer turn away. And a moment later he was forced along in the other's wake to the domes of the once Terran camp. Not just to the camp in general, he discovered a minute later, but to that structure which had housed the com unit linking them with ships cruising the solar lanes and with the patrol. So Thorvald had been right; they needed a Terran to broadcast—to cover their tracks here and lay a trap for the transport.

Shann had no idea how much time he had passed among the Wyverns; the transport with its load of unsuspecting settlers might already be in the system of Circe, plotting a landing orbit around Warlock, broadcasting her recognition signal and a demand for a beam to ride her in. Only, this time the Throgs were out of luck. They had picked up one prisoner who could not help them, even if he wanted to do so. The mysteries of the highly technical installations in this dome were just that to Shann Lantee—complete mysteries. He had not the slightest idea of how to activate the machines, let alone broadcast in the proper code.

A cold spot of terror gathered in his middle, spreading outward through his smarting body. For he was certain that the Throgs would not believe that. They would consider his protestations of ignorance as a stubborn refusal to co-operate. And what would happen to him then would be beyond human endurance. Could he bluff— play for time? But what would that time buy him except

183

to delay the inevitable? In the end, that small hope based on his momentary contact with Thorvald made him decide to try that bluff.

There had been changes in the com dome since the capture of the cap. A squat box on the floor sprouted a collection of tubes from its upper surface. Perhaps that was some Throg equivalent of Terran equipment in place on the wide table facing the door.

The Throg leader clicked into his translator: "You call ship!"

Shann was thrust down into the operator's chair, his bound arms still twisted behind him so that he had to lean forward to keep on the seat at all. Then the Throg who had pushed him there, roughly forced a set of com earphones and speech mike onto his head.

"Call ship!" clicked the alien officer.

So time must be running out. Now was the moment to bluff. Shann shook his head, hoping that the gesture of negation was common to both their species.

"I don't know the code," he said aloud.

The Throg's bulbous eyes gazed at his moving lips. Then the translator was held before the Terran's mouth. Shann repeated his words, heard them reissue as a series of clicks, and waited. So much depended now on the reaction of the beetle-head officer. Would he summarily apply pressure to enforce his order, or would he realize that it was possible that all Terrans did not know that code, and so he could not produce in a captive's head any knowledge that had never been there—with or without physical coercion?

Apparently the latter logic prevailed for the present. The Throg drew the translator back to his mandibles.

"When ship call—you answer—make lip talk your words! Say bad sickness here—need help. Code man dead—you talk in his place. I listen. You say wrong, you die—you die a long time. Hurt bad all that time—"

Clear enough. So he had been able to buy a little time! But how soon before the incoming ship would call? The Throgs seemed to expect it. Shann licked his blistered lips. He was sure that the Throg officer meant exactly what he said in that last grisly threat. Only, would anyone—Throg or human—live very long in this camp if Shann got his warning through? The transport would have been accompanied on the big jump by a patrol cruiser, especially now with Throgs littering deep space the way they were in this sector. Let Shann alert the ship, and the cruiser would know; swift punitive action would be visited on the camp. Throgs could begin to make their helpless prisoner regret his rashness; then all of them would be blotted out together, prisoner and captors alike, when the cruiser came in.

If that was his last chance, he'd play it that way. The Throgs would kill him anyhow, he hadn't the least doubt of that. They kept no long-term Terran prisoners and never had. And at least he could take this nest of devil beetles along with him. Not that the thought did anything to dampen the fear which made him weak and dizzy. Shann Lantee might be tough enough to fight his way out of the Dumps, but to stand up and defy Throgs face-to-face like a video hero was something else. He knew that he could not do any spectacular act; if he could hold out to the end without cracking he would be satisfied.

Two more Throgs entered the dome. They stalked to the far end of the table which held the com equipment, and frequently pausing to consult a Terran work tape set in a reader, they made adjustments to the spotter beam broadcaster. They worked slowly but competently, testing each circuit. Preparing to draw in the Terran transport, holding the large ship until they had it helpless on the ground. The Terran began to wonder how they pro-

185

posed to take the ship over once they did have it on planet.

Transports were armed for ground fighting. Although they rode in on a beam broadcast from a camp, they were prepared for unpleasant surprises on a planet's surface; such were certainly not unknown in the history of Survey. Which meant that the Throgs had in turn some assault weapon they believed superior, for they radiated confidence now. But could they handle a patrol cruiser ready to fight?

The Throg technicians made a last check of the beam, reporting in clicks to the officer. The alien gave an order to Shann's guard before following them out. A loop of wire rope dropped over the Terran's head, tightened about his chest, dragging him back against the chair until he grunted with pain. Two more loops made him secure in a most uncomfortable posture, and then he was left alone in the com dome.

An abortive struggle against the wire rope taught him the folly of such an effort. He was in deep freeze as far as any bodily movement was concerned. Shann closed his eyes, settled to that same concentration he had labored to acquire on the Throg ship. If there was any chance of the Wyvern communication working again, here and now was the time for it!

Again he built his mental picture of Thorvald, as detailed as he had made it in the Throg ship. And with that to the forefront of his mind, Shann strove to pick up the thread which could link them. Was the distance between this camp and the seagirt city of the Wyverns too great? Did the Throgs unconsciously dampen out that mental reaching as the Wyverns had said they did when they had sent him to free the captive in the skull?

Drops gathered in the unkempt tight curls on his head, trickled down to sting on his tender skin. He was bathed in the moisture summoned by an effort as prolonged and severe as if he labored physically under a hot sun at the top speed of which his body was capable.

Thorvald—

Thorvald! But not standing by the window in the Wyvern stronghold! Thorvald with the amethyst of heavy Warlockian foliage at his back. So clear was the new picture that Shann might have stood only a few feet away. Thorvald there, with the wolverines at his side. And behind him sun glinted on the gem-patterned skin of more than one Wyvern.

"Where?"

That demand from the Survey officer, curt, clear—so perfect the word might have rung audibly through the dome.

"The camp!" Shann hurled that back, frantic with fear than once again their contact might fail.

"They want me to call in the transport." He added that.

"How soon?"

"Don't know. They have the guide beam set. I'm to say there's illness here; they know I can't code."

All he could see now was Thorvald's face, intent, the officer's eyes cold sparks of steel, bearing the impress of a will as implacable as a Throg's. Shann added his own decision.

"I'll warn the ship off; they'll send in the patrol."

There was no change in Thorvald's expression. "Hold out as long as you can!"

Cold enough, no promise of help, nothing on which to build hope. Yet the fact that Thorvald was on the move, away from the Wyvern city, meant something. And Shann was sure that thick vegetation could be found only on the mainland. Not only was Thorvald ashore, but there were Wyverns with him. Could the officer have

persuaded the witches of Warlock to foresake their hands-
off policy and join him in an attack on the Throg camp?
No promise, not even a suggestion that the party Shann
had envisioned was moving in his direction. Yet somehow
he believed that they were.

There was a sound from the doorway of the dome.
Shann opened his eyes. There were Throgs entering, one
to go to the guide beam, two heading for his chair. He
closed his eyes again in a last attempt, backed by every
remaining ounce of his energy and will.

"Ship's in range. Throgs here."

Thorvald's face, dimmer now, snapped out while a
blow on Shann's jaw rocked his head cruelly, made his
ears sing, his eyes water. He saw Throgs—Throgs only.
And one held the translator.

"You talk!"

A tri-jointed arm reached across his shoulder, triggered
a lever, pressed a button. The head set cramping his ear
let out a sudden growl of sound—the com was activited.
A claw jammed the mike closer to Shann's lips, but also
slid in range the webbed loop of the translator.

Shann shook his head at the incoming rattle of code.
The Throg with the translator was holding the other head
set close to his own ear pit. And the claws of the guard
came down on Shann's shoulders in a cruel grip, a threat
of future brutality.

The rattle of code continued while Shann thought furi-
ously. This was it! He had to give a warning, and then
the aliens would do to him just what the officer had
threatened. Shann could not seem to think clearly. It was
as if in his efforts to contact Thorvald, he had exhausted
some part of his brain, so that now he was dazed just
when he needed quick wits the most!

This whole scene had a weird unreality. He had seen
its like a thousand times on fiction tapes—the Terran

hero menaced by aliens intent on saving . . . saving . . .

Was it out of one of those fiction tapes he had devoured in the past that Shann recalled that scrap of almost forgotten information?

The Terran began to speak into the mike, for there had come a pause in the rattle of code. He used Terran, not basic, and he shaped the words slowly.

"Warlock calling—trouble—sickness here—com officer dead."

He was interrupted by another burst of code. The claws of his guard twisted into the naked flesh of his shoulders in vicious warning.

"Warlock calling—" he repeated. "Need help—"

"Who are you?"

The demand came in basic. On board the transport they would have a list of every member of the Survey team.

"Lantee." Shann drew a deep breath. He was so conscious of those claws on his shoulders, of what would follow.

"This is Mayday!" he said distinctly, hoping desperately that someone in the control cabin of the ship now in orbit would catch the true meaning of that ancient call of complete disaster. "Mayday—beetles—over and out!"

18. STORM'S ENDING

Shann had no answer from the transport, only the continuing hum of a contact still open between the dome and the control cabin miles above Warlock. The Terran breathed slowly, deeply, felt the claws of the Throg bite his flesh as his chest expanded. Then, as if a knife slashed, the hum of that contact was gone. He had time to know a small flash of triumph. He had done it; he had aroused suspicion in the transport.

When the Throg officer clicked to the alien manning the landing beam, Shann's exultation grew. The beetle-head must have accepted that cut in communication as normal; he was still expecting the Terran ship to drop neatly into his claws.

But Shann's respite was to be very short, only timed by a few breaths. The Throg at the riding beam was watching the indicators. Now he reported to his superior, who swung back to face the prisoner. Although Shann could read no expression on the beetle's face, he did not need any clue to the other's probable emotions. Knowing that his captive had somehow tricked him, the alien would now proceed relentlessly to put into effect the measures he had threatened.

How long before the patrol cruiser would planet? That crew was used to alarms, and their speed was three or four times greater than that of the bulkier transports. If the Throgs didn't scatter now, before they could be caught in one attack . . .

The wire rope which held Shann clamped to the chair was loosened, and he set his teeth against the pain of restored circulation. This was nothing compared to what he faced; he knew that. They jerked him to his feet, faced him toward the outer door, and propelled him through it with a speed and roughness indicative of their feelings.

The hour was close to dusk and Shann glanced wistfully at promising shadows, though he had given up hope of rescue by now. If he could just get free of his guards, he could at least give the beetle-heads a good run.

He saw that the camp was deserted. There was no sign about the domes that any Throgs sheltered there. In fact,

Shann saw no aliens at all except those who had come from the com dome with him. Of course! The rest must be in ambush, waiting for the transport to planet. What about the Throg ship or ships? Those must have been hidden also. And the only hiding place for them would be aloft. There was a chance that the Throgs had so flung away their chance for any quick retreat.

Yes, the aliens could scatter over the countryside and so escape the first blast from the cruiser. But they would simply maroon themselves to be hunted down by patrol landing parties who would comb the territory. The beetles could so prolong their lives for a few hours, maybe a few days, but they were really ended on that moment when the transport cut communication. Shann was sure that the officer, at least, understood that.

The Terran was dragged away from the domes toward the river down which he and Thovald had once escaped. Moving through the dusk in parallel lines, he caught sight of other Throg squads, well armed, marching in order to suggest that they were not yet alarmed. However, he had been right about the ships—there were no flyers grounded on the improvised field.

Shann made himself as much of a burden as he could. At the best, he could so delay the guards entrusted with his safekeeping; at the worst, he could earn for himself a quick ending by blaster which would be better than the one they had for him. He went limp, falling forward into the trampled grass. There was an exasperated click from the Throg who had been herding him, and the Terran tried not to flinch from a sharp kick delivered by a clawed foot.

Feigning unconsciousness, the Terran listened to the unintelligible clicks exchanged by Throgs standing over him. His future depended now on how deep lay the alien officer's anger. If the beetle-head wanted to carry out his earlier threats, he would have to order Shann's transportation by the fleeing force. Otherwise his life might well end here and now.

Claws hooked once more on Shann. He was boosted up on the horny carapace of a guard, the bonds on his arms taken off and his numbed hands brought forward, to be held by his captor so that he lay helpless, a cloak over the other's hunched shoulders.

The ghost flares of bushes and plants blooming in the gathering twilight gave a limited light to the scene. There was no way of counting the number of Throgs on the move. But Shann was sure that all the enemy ships must have been emptied except for skeleton crews, and perhaps others had been ferried in from their hidden base somewhere in Circe's system.

He could only see a little from his position on the Throg's back, but ahead a ripple of beetle bodies slipped over the bank of the river cut. The aliens were working their way into cover, fitting into the dapple shadows with a skill which argued a long practice in such elusive maneuvers. Did they plan to try to fight off a cruiser attack? That was pure madness. Or, Shann wondered, did they intend to have the Terrans met by one of their own major ships somewhere well above the surface of Warlock?

His bearer turned away from the stream cut, carrying Shann out into that field which had first served the Terrans as a landing strip, then offered the same service to the Throgs. They passed two more parties of aliens on the move, manhandling with them bulky objects the Terran could not identify. Then he was dumped unceremoniously to the hard earth, only to lie there a few seconds before he was flopped over on a framework which grated unpleasantly against his raw shoulders, his wrists and ankles being made fast so that his body was spread-eagled. There was a click of orders; the frame was raised and dropped with a jarring movement into a base, and he was held erect, once more facing the Throg with the translator. This was it! Shann began to regret every small chance he had had to end more cleanly. If he had attacked one of the guards, even with his hands bound, he might have flustered the Throg into retaliatory blaster fire.

Fear made a thicker fog about him than the green mist of the illusion. Only this was no illusion. Shann stared at the Throg officer with sick eyes, knowing that no one ever quite believes that a last evil will strike at him, that he had clung to a hope which had no existence.

"Lantee!"

The call burst in his head with a painful force. His dazed attention was outwardly on the alien with the translator, but that inner demand had given him a shock.

"Here! Thorvald? Where?"

The other struck in again with an urgent demand singing through Shann's brain.

"Give us a fix point—away from camp but not too far. Quick!"

A fix point—what did the Survey officer mean? A fix point . . . For some reason Shann thought of the ledge on which he had lain to watch the first Throg attack. And the picture of it was etched on his mind as clearly as memory could paint it.

"Thorvald—" Again his voice and his mind call were echoes of each other. But this time he had no answer. Had that demand meant Thorvald and the Wyverns were moving in, putting to use the strange distance-erasing power the witches of Warlock could use by desire? But why had they not come sooner? And what could they hope to accomplish against the now scattered but certainly unbroken enemy forces? The Wyverns had not

been able to turn their power against one injured Throg
—by their own accounting—how could they possibly
cope with well-armed and alert aliens in the field?

"You die—slow—" The Throg officer clicked, and the
emotionless, toneless translation was all the more daunt-
ing for that lack of color. "Your people come—see—"

So that was the reason they had brought him to the
landing field. He was to furnish a grisly warning to the
crew of the cruiser. However, there the Throgs were
making a bad mistake if they believed that his death by
any ingenious method could scare off Terran retaliation.

"I die—you follow—" Shann tried to make that promise emphatic.

Did the Throg officer expect the Terran to beg for his
life or a quick death? Again he made his threat—straight
into the web, hearing it split into clicks.

"Perhaps," the Throg returned. "But you die the first."

"Get to it!" Shann's voice scaled up. He was close to
the ragged edge, and the last push toward the breaking
point had not been the Throg speech, but that message
from Thorvald. If the Survey officer was going to make
any move in the mottled dusk, it would have to be
soon.

Mottled dusk . . . The Throgs had moved a little away
from him. Shann looked beyond them to the perimeter of
the cleared field, not really because he expected to see
any rescuers break from cover there. And when he did
see a change, Shann thought his own sight was at fault.

Those splotches of waxy light which marked certain
trees, bushes, and scrubby ground-hugging plants were
spreading, running together in pools. And from those
center cores of concentrated glow, tendrils of mist lazily
curled out, as a many-armed creature of the sea might
allow its appendages to float in the water which supported it. Tendrils crossed, met, and thickened. There

was a growing river of eerie light which spread, again resembling a sea wave licking out onto the field. And where it touched, unlike the wave, it did not retreat, but lapped on. Was he actually seeing that? Shann could not be sure.

Only the gray light continued to build, faster now, its speed of advance matching its increase in bulk. Shann somehow connected it with the evil of illusion. If it was real, there was a purpose behind it.

There was an aroused clicking from the Throgs. A blaster bolt cracked, its spiteful, sickly yellow slicing into the nearest tongue of gray. But that luminous fog engulfed the blast and was not dispelled. Shann forced his head around against the support which held him. The mist crept across the field from all quarters, walling them in.

Running at the ungainly lope which was their best effort at speed were half a dozen Throgs emerging from the river section. Their attitude suggested panic-stricken flight, and when one tripped on some unseen obstruction and went down—to fall beneath a descending tongue of phosphorescence—he uttered a strange high-pitched squeal, thin and faint, but still a note of complete, mindless terror.

The Throgs surrounding Shann were firing at the fog, first with precision, then raggedly, as their bolts did nothing to cut that opaque curtain drawing in about them. From inside that mist came other sounds—noises, calls, and cries all alien to him, and perhaps also to the Throgs. There were shapes barely to be discerned through the swirls; perhaps some were Throgs in flight. But certainly others were non-Throg in outline. And the Terran was sure that at least three of those shapes, all different, had been in pursuit of one fleeing. Throg, heading him off from that small open area still holding about Shann.

For the Throgs were being herded in from all sides—the handful who had come from the river, the others who had brought Shann there. And the action of the mist was pushing them into a tight knot. Would they eventually turn on him, wanting to make sure of their prisoner before they made a last stand against whatever lurked in the fog? To Shann's continued relief the aliens seemed to have forgotten him. Even when one cowered back against the very edge of the frame on which the Terran was bound, the beetle-head did not look at this helpless prey.

They were firing wildly, with desperation in every heavy thrust of bolt. Then one Throg threw down his blaster, raised his arms over his head, and voicing the same high wail uttered by his comrade-in-arms earlier, he ran straight into the mist where a shape materialized closed in behind him, cutting him off from his fellows.

That break demoralized the others. The Throg commander burned down two of his company with his blaster, but three more broke past him to the fog. One of the remaining party reversed his blaster, swung the stock against the officer's carapace, beating him to his knees before the attacker raced on into the billows of the mist. Another threw himself on the ground and lay there, pounding his claws against the baked earth. While a remaining two continued with stolid precision to fire at the lurking shapes which could only be half seen; and a third helped the officer to his feet.

The Throg commander reeled back against the frame, his musky body scent filling Shann's nostrils. But he, too, paid no attention to the Terran, though his horny arms scraped across Shann's. Holding both of his claws to his head, he staggered on, to be engulfed by a new arm of the fog.

Then, as if the swallowing of the officer had given the

...ist a fresh appetite, the wan light waved in a last vast
illow over the clear area about the frame. Shann felt its
...bstance cold, slimy, on his skin. This was a deadly
...reath of un-life.

He was weakened, sapped of strength, so that he hung
...n his bounds, his head lolling forward on his breast.
Warmth pressed against him, a warm wet touch on his
...old skin, a sensation of friendly concern in his mind.
...hann gasped, found that he was no longer filling his
...ungs with that chill staleness which was the breath of
...he fog. He opened his eyes, struggling to raise his head.
...he gray light had retreated, but though a Throg blaster
...y close to his feet, another only a yard beyond, there
...vas no sign of the aliens.

Instead, standing on their hind feet to press against
...im in a demand for his attention, were the wolverines.
...nd seeing them, Shann dared to believe that the impos-
...ible could be true; somehow he was safe.

He spoke. And Taggi and Togi answered with eager
...vhines. The mist was withdrawing more slowly than it
...ad come. Here and there things lay very still on the
...round.

"Lantee!"

This time the call came not into his mind but out of the
...ir. Shann made an effort at reply which was close to a
...roak.

"Over here!"

A new shape in the fog was moving with purpose to-
...vard him. Thorvald strode into the open, sighted Shann,
...nd began to run.

"What did they—?" he began.

Shann wanted to laugh, but the sound which issued
...rom his dry throat was very little like mirth. He strug-
...led helplessly until he managed to get out some words
...vhich made sense.

". . . hadn't started in on me yet. You were just i
time."

Thorvald loosened the wires which held the younge
man to the frame and stood ready to catch him as h
slumped forward. And the officer's hold wiped away th
last clammy residue of the mist. Though he did not seer
able to keep on his feet, Shann's mind was clear.

"What happened?" he demanded.

"The power." Thorvald was examining him hastily bu
with attention for every cut and bruise. "The beetle
heads didn't really get to work on you—"

"Told you that," Shann said impatiently. "But wha
brought that fog and got the Throgs?"

Thorvald smiled grimly. The ghostly light was fadin
as the fog retreated, but Shann could see well enough t
note that around the other's neck hung one of th
Wyvern disks.

"It was a variation of the veil of illusion. You face
your memories under the influence of that; so did I. Bu
it would seem that the Throgs had ones worse tha
either of us could produce. You can't play the role o
thug all over the galaxy and not store up in the subcor
scious a fine line of private fears and remembered ene
mies. We provided the means for releasing those, an
they simply raised their own devils to order. Neates
justice ever rendered. It seems that the 'power' has
big kick—in a different way—when a Terran will man
ages to spark it."

"And you did?"

"I made a small beginning. Also I had the full backing
of the Elders, and a general staff of Wyverns in support
In a way I helped to provide a channel for their concen
tration. Alone they can work 'magic'; with us they ca
spread out into new fields. Tonight we hunted Throgs a
a united team—most successfully."

"But they wouldn't go after the one in the skull."

"No. Direct contact with a Throg mind appears to
nortcircuit them. I did the contacting; they fed me what
needed. We have the answer to the Throgs now—one
nswer." Thorvald looked back over the field where those
odies lay so still. "We can kill Throgs. Maybe someday
c can learn another trick—how to live with them." He
eturned abruptly to the present. "You did contact the
ransport?"

Shann explained what had happened in the com dome.
I think when the ship broke contact that way they un-
erstood."

"We'll take it that they did, and be on the move."
horvald helped Shann to his feet. "If a cruiser berths
ere shortly, I don't propose to be under its tail flames
rhen it sets down."

The cruiser came. And a mop-up squad patrolled out-
ard from the reclaimed camp, picked up two living
hrogs, both wandering witlessly. But Shann only heard
f that later. He slept, so deep and dreamlessly that when
e roused he was momentarily dazed.

A Survey uniform—with a cadet's badges—lay across
ne wall seat facing his bunk in the barracks he had left
. . how many days or weeks before? The garments fitted
rell enough, but he removed the insignia to which he
ras not entitled. When he ventured out he saw half a
ozen troopers of the patrol, together with Thorvald,
ratching the cruiser lift again into the morning sky.

Taggi and Togi, trailing leashes, galloped out of no-
rhere to hurl themselves at him in uproarious welcome.
nd Thorvald must have heard their eager whines even
hough the blast of the ship, for he turned and waved
hann to join him.

"Where is the cruiser going?"

"To punch a Throg base out of this system," Thorval answered. "They located it—on Witch."

"But we're staying on here?"

Thorvald glanced at him oddly. "There won't be a settlement now. But we have to establish a condition embassy post. And the patrol has left a guard."

Embassy post. Shann digested that. Yes, of cours Thorvald, because of his close contact with the Wyverr would be left here for the present to act as liaison office in-charge.

"We don't propose," the other was continuing, " allow to lapse any contact with the one intelligent alie race we have discovered who can furnish us with fu time partnership to our mutual benefit. And there mustr be any bungling here!"

Shann nodded. That made sense. As soon as possib Warlock would witness the arrival of another team, o slated this time to the cultivation of an alien friendsh and alliance, rather than preparation for Terran colonis Would they keep him on? He supposed not; the wolve ines' usefulness was no longer apparent.

"Don't you know your regulations?" There was a sna in Thorvald's demand which startled Shann. He glance up, discovered the other surveying him critically. "You'r not in uniform—"

"No, sir," he admitted. "I couldn't find my own kit."

"Where are your badges?"

Shann's hand went up to the marks left when he had carefully ripped off the insignia.

"My badges? I have no rank," he replied, bewildere

"Every team carries at least one cadet on strength."

Shann flushed. There had been one cadet on this tean why did Thorvald want to remember that?

"Also," the other's voice sounded remote, "there can appointments made in the field—for cause. Those a pointments are left to the discretion of the officer-in-charge, and they are never questioned. I repeat, you are not in uniform, Lantee. You will make the necessary alteration and report to me at headquarters dome. As sole representatives of Terra here we have a matter of protocol to be discussed with our witches, and they have a right to expect punctuality from a pair of warlocks, so get going!"

Shann still stood, staring incredulously at the officer. Then Thorvald's official severity vanished in a smile which was warm and real.

"Get going," he ordered once more, "before I have to log you for inattention to orders."

Shann turned, nearly stumbling over Taggi, and then ran back to the barracks in quest of some very important bits of braid he hoped he could find in a hurry.

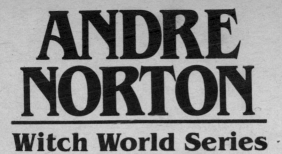

ANDRE NORTON

Witch World Series

Enter the Witch World for a feast of
adventure and enchantment, magic and
sorcery.

89705	**Witch World**	$1.95
87875	**Web of the Witch World**	$1.95
80805	**Three Against the Witch World**	$1.95
87323	**Warlock of the Witch World**	$1.95
77555	**Sorceress of the Witch World**	$1.95
94254	**Year of the Unicorn**	$1.95
82356	**Trey of Swords**	$1.95
95490	**Zarsthor's Bane** (illustrated)	$1.95